The Cut Above

— A NOVEL —

DAN RAGINS

PAGE PUBLISHING, INC.
Conneaut Lake, PA

First originally published by Page Publishing 2019

ISBN 978-1-64584-589-8 (pbk)
ISBN 978-1-64584-588-1 (digital)

Printed in the United States of America

Chapter One

Jamie Duncan anticipated the sensation of falling through space. He never forgot the last time it happened. He was twelve years old at Chicago's old Riverview amusement park. His friends had dared him to ride the parachutes. He took the dare and, at the apex of his rise to the top of the ride, gave a macho wave to the boys below. Then there was a loud *click* followed by an extraordinary, almost eerie sensation in his balls as he free-fell through space. Fear penetrated his being for the few seconds before the parachute opened and controlled his descent to earth.

He couldn't quite believe that now, a day before his fortieth birthday, he would be bungee jumping toward a river ten stories below with only a piece of elasticized rubber keeping him from certain death. His wife, Emma, knew him to be a daredevil in other parts of his life and had encouraged him to give it a try. His high school friend Mohammed owned the bungee-jump concession and assured him he would be safe...even gave him a friendly dare so he could prove he wasn't "chicken."

As Jamie stood on the bridge railing, his mind brought back the never-forgotten sensation in his groin from the parachutes.

"This is it, honey," giggled Emma. "Give me a kiss, big boy, before you take your *leap of faith*."

He bent down far enough to give her a quick peck on the lips and then stood to prepare himself.

"Ready if you are," said Mohammed.

"Guess I am, pal," responded Jamie, "but you'd better be sure about this piece of rubber."

"I am sure," came the response.

Jamie jumped. As he approached the water at eighty miles an hour, all on the bridge heard a terrible *snap* as the rubber curled and hurtled itself toward the water, following Jamie toward the rocks hidden just below the surface.

Chapter Two

This is the tale of three young souls—Jamie Duncan, Emma Steele, and their close friend Mohammed Amsur. They were, in several ways, special among the hundreds of ordinary students at Salmon High, located in the small rural town of Salmon, Idaho, near the wild middle fork of the Salmon River.

Special because they were the smartest, the best-looking, and the wittiest. The only trouble was that Jamie and Mohammed were in love with the same girl—Emma. What a sweetheart. Everyone loved Emma—the teachers, the principal, everyone's parents, and of course, virtually everyone at school. But it was just Jamie and Mohammed who had that special kind of romantic love for her. And that's where the story begins.

It started on the first day of their first semester in high school. They had never set eyes on one another before that day. Mohammed entered his first-period classroom before the others and plunked himself down in the back row. He was never one to seek attention; in fact, he avoided it like the plague. He was introverted and very aware that he was different. Of Iranian descent, he had a full head of curly black hair, darker skin than the others, and had been raised as a Muslim. Clearly, he was the only such student at Salmon High and one of the few such people in Idaho in 1969.

His family had come to Idaho just two months before school began. They had been in Canada, where they had emigrated from Iran when he was only five. After eight years, his father had been granted a green card by the US government, and they moved south of the border. His dad was able to buy a small dry-cleaning shop in Salmon. It was a start for them, and they found themselves warmly welcomed by this surprisingly friendly community.

As he sat in his seat at the rear of the room, Mohammed observed his new classmates as they entered. The fourth person through the door was Jamie Duncan. He was to be the inevitable "it man" of the class. He was the tallest, most handsome, and smartest, not to mention the best athlete among them—a star on the Salmon Savages football team. He was also Mohammed's social opposite. An extrovert of the first order, most who met him initially found him to be pushy and a bit of a wise guy. It really took a while to get to know him, but once they did, people quickly realized there was much more substance there than bluster.

Jamie sat down next to Mohammed and immediately introduced himself. Jamie was a Chicago boy. He was the only big-city kid in town, which gave him a leg up on all his country bumpkin classmates. He really knew much more about life than a boy of fourteen would be inclined to know in the backwaters of Idaho.

He knew a bit about girls too. When the fifth person entered the classroom, it just happened to be Emma Steele. When Mohammed saw her, his jaw just dropped. So did

Jamie's. Here was the quintessential small-town, all-American girl with a face and figure that belied her youth. She had natural blond hair, a smile that beamed, and a personality so genuine and upbeat nobody could resist her.

While Mohammed sat there gawking, Jamie waved to her as though he had known her forever. He motioned for her to come over and sit next to him. In just minutes, the two of them were engaged in a nonstop conversation. Occasionally, they would include Mohammed in their dialogue. After offering a word or two in response, he would usually find himself out again, looking in on their instantly established world.

This was to be the tone of their four years of high school. Jamie and Emma became friends on that first day and a couple soon after. Mohammed was always part of the threesome but also inevitably the odd man out—a fact that made him envious of Jamie in the extreme. Mohammed knew Jamie and Emma loved each other but felt Jamie's feelings for her could never be as strong or true as his own. The difference, of course, was that Jamie was living in reality while "Mo," as he was now known to most, was in his own little fantasy world.

A word about Emma. A real sweetheart. She came from a great family that was deeply devoted to the outdoors. Her dad worked as a fishing guide in the warmer months, and her mother as a rafting guide on the river. In the winter, they operated a cross-country skiing service, and both were volunteer firefighters throughout the year. Coming from this warm, interactive environment, Emma grew up with a strong, positive attitude and longed one day to be a teacher to first graders and a mom to as many kids as she could handle.

Over their four years of high school, Jamie and Emma became a real couple. Mo watched from the sidelines, good friends with both, but with ever-growing jealousy of Jamie's relationship with Emma. Mo dated during those four years, and while he was generally accepted, no girls really wanted to go steady with a boy who looked like an outsider. It wasn't until his senior year, when another family of Iranian immigrants came to Salmon at the urging of his dad, that he met a girl who was really interested in him.

High school passed quickly. Their friendships grew stronger, and they all did well in school. Jamie and Emma, however, were exceptional both academically and socially. Jamie won a full scholarship to Stanford, while Emma, who couldn't have afforded college without it, gained a full ride to UC Berkeley. This would allow the couple to easily see a lot of each other as the schools were not too far apart in Northern California.

Mo, on the other hand, did not get a scholarship and could not afford college on his own. Instead, he went to work with his dad after graduation and soon contributed modern ideas that helped grow the family business.

Shortly after Labor Day in 1973, Jamie and Emma, accompanied by their parents, moved into their rooms at their respective schools. Emma was to be in a standard dorm room with a roommate she had never met, Sarah. The two never became very close. Sarah was a brilliant intellect but totally void of a personality. In their four years together, they got along by simply keeping out of each other's way.

Jamie, on the other hand, joined Sigma Chi and was quickly absorbed into the fraternity party scene. While he and Emma now saw each other on most weekends, partying never seemed to stop for Jamie. He was "forced" to date other girls at a number of weekday events and had a sexual relationship with two of them. Nothing serious, just fun. Somehow he managed to conceal these "meaningless" relationships from Emma, who he met most often in Berkeley.

In their sophomore year, the two of them began to talk more seriously of marriage, and by the end of that year, their physical relationship had progressed from years of heavy petting to sleeping together. From then on, Jamie stopped seeing anyone but Emma.

After four years of college, Jamie and Emma came to the logical point of marriage. Quite by chance, their separate graduations fell on the same day. Their parents, who had become close friends as a result of their children's relationship, planned a wonderful postgraduation dinner party in San Francisco. It was at this party that the kids added to their parents' delight with an announcement that they were officially engaged and were planning to wed as soon as possible.

July 3, 1977, was a warm day and perfect for an outdoor wedding in Salmon. The Steeles and Duncans combined their funds to give their kids a great start. In this part of the country, that didn't mean a fancy hotel with elegant food and wine; instead, it meant a ceremony held in the gazebo located in the town square. Relatives and friends supplied the food, which was served cafeteria style; soft drinks and beer were the quaffs of choice. Jamie's younger brother Ted, a part-time DJ, provided music for the event. What was most important to Jamie and Emma was that all their friends and family could attend.

July 14, 1977, was the last day of their honeymoon. On returning home, their mail revealed two new job opportunities. Emma was thrilled to find out her own first-grade teacher, now seventy years old, had decided to retire. The principal, who had known Emma all her life and was aware of both her exceptional academic achievements and lifelong desire to teach first grade, offered her the job she had always yearned for. Jamie, on the other hand, received a notice he was expecting, but not quite so soon. He had joined the ROTC at Stanford and was required to serve two years in the army. He had thought he would have at least a few more months with his bride before being called up. As it turned out, he had only two weeks before he would be reporting for duty.

Chapter Three

Jamie's degree was in business. When he first began at Stanford, he envisioned himself leaving small-town Idaho and taking Emma with him to a fast-paced life on Wall Street.

Understandably, small-town Emma didn't see things quite that way, and after four years in college of back and forth on the subject, Jamie finally agreed to stay in Salmon. This left him, however, without his plan...one that he had been anticipating for years. The army gave him two years to think about his future.

Shortly after basic training and his being awarded the gold bars of a second lieutenant, Jamie was assigned to a station in the Pentagon with army intelligence. For a change, the army got it right. Not only did he have the brains for this work, but he also loved the intrigue. Initially, he was sent to a section where they decoded messages, mostly from Russia and China. Later, he was involved in one of the few spying efforts conducted jointly by the army and the CIA. Near the end of his two years, he acted as an internal spy, checking on others in the military when Washington had concerns over potential leaks. It was all fascinating for him, and his performance was exemplary. When he was about to be discharged, the army approached him about staying and offered him a jump from his current rank of captain to that of major.

During his time in service, Jamie had been home a total of just six weeks. Putting in that kind of time away from home caused considerable stress with his new bride who, while loving her first graders, longed for a husband on the home front. While Emma was generally a patient and understanding woman, the idea of being a career army wife was, to her, out of the question. The army gave Jamie a week of leave to see if he could change her mind. He didn't succeed in this mission but did manage something else. While home, Emma became pregnant.

Jamie was torn. He had spent two years at a job he loved and a promising career in the military, and now, just weeks after returning home, lacked direction. While he was thrilled with the idea of becoming a father, he was not sure what he would do with himself or how he would pay for his new life in Salmon.

Two months passed. Emma was in heaven, thinking only of motherhood and having her man back home. Jamie, however, was going crazy with boredom, as there was nothing of longterm interest for him in Salmon. Every day, Jamie would wait for the postman to bring the mail and a copy of the *New York Times*. He developed a habit of scanning the help wanted ads. As he was about to begin his daily ritual, the phone rang. On the other end was his closest army buddy, Jay Collins, a fellow that had mentored him for a year when he came to Washington but who then left the service six months before Jamie's tour ended.

After fifteen minutes of rehashing the "old days," Jay began to talk about his new job with the CIA. He went on to tell Jamie how he (like Jamie) had liked the work in army intelligence but needed a bit more adventure. While still in army intel, he had an assignment in conjunction with the CIA. After spending a couple of months with the spy agency, he decided that the excitement he saw there was just what he was looking for.

"Hold on," said Jamie. "You know me. I would love that kind of thing. Why didn't you tell me what you were up to before?"

"Well," replied Jay, "you were still in the army while I was going through training. And then we sort of lost contact. This afternoon, I was in Boise waiting for a flight and remembered that you lived in this neck of the woods, so I called to catch up. However, if you'd be interested, I can tell you that they just put out an internal memo that they're looking for some new people. However, from what you just told me about your wife expecting and wanting you to be on the home front, I'm not so sure she would be in favor of this kind of work. What do you think? Could you convince her?"

"Well, you have a point, but I'm going crazy here. Why don't you give me a contact at Langley, and I'll start the ball rolling? If I apply and they ask me to take an interview, I'll see what I can do to convince Emma that this could be the right thing for me."

The next day, Jamie spoke to the contact at CIA headquarters. His military experience plus a word from Jay as his reference gave him a leg up. When the people at Langley finally received and took a look at his application, along with his résumé featuring his outstanding grades at Stanford, they immediately faxed him a letter giving him a date and time for an appointment at Langley in two weeks. Jamie must have read it a dozen times before it truly sank in.

Jamie Duncan, US spy, he thought to himself. He was thrilled until Emma came home.

He quickly ditched the letter, kissed her hello, and began to think about what words he could use to convince her this was right for both of them. It would be a hard sell.

He waited until dinner was over. As Emma washed the dishes, and he dried, he casually mentioned he had finally found a job prospect that really interested him. She smiled and asked him to tell her about it. When the fatal letters *CIA* passed his lips, she froze.

"You're teasing me, aren't you?" she asked, almost in a whisper, her lips tightening over her perfect teeth.

"Well, I guess I knew you might not be thrilled with this idea, but the truth is that it's the kind of work I'd love. But look, I haven't even been offered the job. It's just an interview, so please keep an open mind until I find out what it's all about."

Emma wanted to scream but held herself back. She had seen how unhappy Jamie had been since coming home and decided he should at least have a chance to get it out of his system. Surely, she thought, with a baby coming soon, he wouldn't want to be away from home.

The appointment was perfect. The job description was exactly what he was hoping for.

After one year of basic training, he would receive a few months of advanced training before becoming a spy in the field. Training would be on the East Coast. He would still be in-country when the baby was born and was told he would have R&R time to return home for two weeks after the birth. Now all he had to do was convince Emma—a challenge greater to overcome, perhaps, than the KGB.

Chapter Four

"I tried it, and you saw what happened," he said. "I came home, looked for meaningful work here, and found nothing. Four years at Stanford Business School, and for what? There's simply not a job here that will work for me. I know you don't want to leave home, and I understand you have your dream job, your friends, and family, and our baby on the way. I realize I have most of those things as well, but there's simply no career here for me, and I'm not planning to retire at the ripe old age of twenty-four. What else would you have me do?"

Emma stayed quiet. He could see her pondering an answer. She wished she had a good one but didn't. Finally, she broke her silence.

"Jamie, I love you more than you can imagine. I think you know that. When I learned I was pregnant, I was the happiest person in Salmon, knowing we would be here together for it. I know I can't blame you for wanting a meaningful career, and I appreciate your willingness to move back home instead of going to New York. I know you tried to keep me happy by doing that for me, but now I feel stuck. I know in my heart that it's not fair to keep you here while I just have my way. Yet I think of our baby growing up with an often absent father and of us possibly growing apart without you being here. Give me a day to sort it out in my head and let's talk again tomorrow after dinner."

Jamie agreed. He also knew that this girl he had loved, seemingly forever, was always fair-minded, giving, and willing to consider both sides of any situation. He felt he had a chance. And that's the way it turned out.

"Thanks, honey," he said as he held her close the next night. "It will be a tough year, but I'll be back for the baby's birth, and we'll take it a step at a time from there."

"Just know, Jamie, that I love you dearly and that I pray for your happiness and your safety. We've been together for nearly half of our still-young lives, and I never want it to end. But I also want it to be real and close and not an arm's-length marriage. Please promise me you'll do everything you can to make that happen."

"I promise, my love," Jamie said. Then he kissed her, and they made sweet, beautiful love.

Chapter Five

Two weeks later, Jamie was packed and headed to Langley. From there, he would join a half dozen other recruits and move on to the secret CIA training facility. Jamie bonded quickly with four other guys while they all navigated the tough training course—Bob Craig, Jeff Allen, Skip Green, and Herb Harrison.

Of this group, Jamie had, by far, the most experience due to his army days. Many of the class lessons were in areas where he had firsthand experience. He combined his past knowledge with new subjects, such as unique technical devices (à la James Bond) and compressed classes in critical languages. He loved these new challenges and often found himself tutoring his buddies in areas he already knew well, such as secret codes and interrogation techniques. He was, however, the type of guy who became so involved with his work that he could be inclined to neglect other important details…such as his pregnant wife.

In the first month of training, Jamie managed to call Emma once each week. During the second month, he called on only one occasion. So while he was having a ball, stress began to build in Emma. At the end of the second month, Colonel Jones, head of the training facility, called Jamie into his office. Jamie took one look at his face and knew something was terribly wrong.

"Sit down, Mr. Duncan," he said quietly. "I'm afraid I have some unfortunate news for you."

"My god, sir, have I done something wrong? I thought my training was going very well."

"Your training, young man, has been exceptional. But it's not that part of your life where the trouble lies. I just received a call from your mother. It seems your wife has suffered a miscarriage. While that, in itself, is obviously unfortunate, there have apparently been some severe complications. Your mother asked that you call her right away for the full details. You can use my phone. I'll step out so you can have privacy. Just let me know when you're through."

"Thank you, sir. I guess I'm in a bit of shock. I'll call right now." Jamie's mother answered the phone on the first ring.

"Mom, what happened? Please tell me Emma's going to be okay!"

"Well, honey, she'll be okay. But there were complications so serious that they required a hysterectomy. In other words, she won't be able to have children in the future. You know how important a large family was to Emma. The trauma of it all has her usual upbeat manner way down. And while I hate to say it, I think the problems stem from stress caused, at least in part, by your lack of contact with her. She was so upset that you called her only once in the past month. She was thinking that you didn't care about her any longer. When women are pregnant, they become more sensitive about so many things. But thoughts of losing her husband's love in her state became a crushing blow."

"Oh my god," Jamie replied. "I've just been so involved here I guess I've gotten carried away. But you know, I would certainly hope she would know that I couldn't love anyone or anything more than her. Mom, let me see if I can get a couple of days' leave to come home. They normally won't allow it, but in this case, I may have a chance. I'll call you back."

Jamie left the office and crossed the hall to where his supervisor was reading a report.

"Sir, I can't believe what has happened. Did my mom tell you all the details?"

"She did."

"Given the circumstances, I must request a couple of days to go home to look after my wife. She's everything to me, and I guess I'm to blame for at least part of the situation. I still can't believe this has happened."

"The fact is we have one of our planes heading for Boise on a mission. It leaves in two hours. Be on it. You'll have seventy-two hours to straighten out your personal affairs. That same plane will be headed back here on Monday next. I'll expect you to be aboard."

"Thank you, sir. I can't tell you how much I appreciate your consideration."

Chapter Six

Being left out reminded Mo a bit of the first day of high school when Jamie was totally absorbed in his conversation with Emma. Now, however, Jamie's fascination—or more accurately, his obsession—was with becoming a spy. This time, it wasn't Mo who was being left out in the cold…it was Emma. Now that she had lost not only the baby but also the prospect of ever having her own children, she sank into a deep depression.

Jamie did what he could in his brief time at home. He apologized profusely for his inattention, swore there never was another woman in his life, and tried to assure Emma that all would be well once his training was over. Emma wouldn't leave Salmon, and while Jamie did call regularly and returned home for an early R&R, it was Mo who really kept Emma going and brought her out of her funk and back to being the Emma he had always known.

You might say he became her "husband in residence." Even before the miscarriage, they were out together at least once or twice a week and managed to talk almost every day. One of their main topics of conversation had always been children, and now it had become how adopting a baby would be a wonderful thing for Emma to consider when Jamie next returned on leave. It was a subject that gave her reason for hope and, at least for the moment, made her happy.

Chapter Seven

When Jamie finally finished CIA training in 1980, he and Emma had been married for almost three years. In that time, they hadn't spent even four months together. Emma was hoping he would somehow be assigned to a location in the States, preferably in the northwest. When she heard the words "Saudi Arabia," she was devastated once again. While Jamie offered to take her along with him, he told her just how limited her life would be there, where women had minimal freedom at best.

The assignment was for two years, with four weeks R&R each year. She cried endlessly. Jamie, without other options, apologized repeatedly while he prepared to leave. The night before Jamie was to fly out, Emma sat Jamie down and told him their marriage had become a very bad and painful joke. She said it was ridiculous to call them a couple when they were almost never together. Add to that, the fact that she could never have a baby, and she felt they should consider Jamie's two years in Saudi Arabia a more formal "trial separation." If, after that time, they couldn't be together and make it work, Emma said they should just get a divorce and start over.

Jamie was stunned when she said, "trial separation." When she used the word "divorce," he went into shock.

He sat a few moments without a response. He then begged Emma to be patient. He said if he couldn't get a reasonable assignment after Saudi Arabia, he would quit and come back to the States. Anyway, that's the way they left it. Now they were technically separated. If she ever felt alone before, it was much more so now. In a strange way, she felt guilty for pushing things over the edge. On the other hand, she felt justified in what she had done.

After Emma related the discussion to Mo, he had to process this turn of events before making any moves. He knew what he wanted, and with Jamie thousands of miles away, he knew it was plausible. He just had to figure out how to make it happen.

Chapter Eight

There had never been so forlorn a face on Emma as the day she and Mo watched Jamie's plane take off from the military section at Boise Airport. As the plane disappeared over the horizon, there was a numb stare of disbelief in Emma's eyes. She then turned to Mo, put her head on his shoulder, and sobbed quietly until she could no more.

They walked slowly back to the car. He had expected sadness, but this gray day cast an emotional pall that demanded quiet. Neither of them uttered a word for miles until Mo spotted a favorite place of theirs in North Fork, a town just a short ride from Salmon. It was a friendly, upbeat pub where the locals gathered on weekend nights for lively conversation, a bit of karaoke, and some simple but delicious pub food. Without a word, Mo pulled off the highway and parked in front. When the car stopped, Emma snapped out of what was obviously deep thought about her life situation.

"Why are we stopping?" she queried. "I don't think I can handle this place today of all days."

"On the contrary, my dearest friend, what you need more than anything is to bring yourself out of the doldrums and back to being the most wonderful, upbeat girl I've ever known. A little drink, a few songs, and some solid food to rejuvenate your body and soul…and I'm going to make sure you have them all."

Reluctantly, Emma allowed herself to be coaxed out of the car. The tears were gone, but the sadness lingered. When Mo opened the door to the pub, the noise from the band jarred her senses, and for the first time in weeks, her lips parted in the beautiful smile that captivated all who had the privilege of seeing it. This was the moment when Emma Duncan began to heal.

Chapter Nine

Jamie landed in Riyadh in the late morning. He had taken a sleeping pill, hoping to keep himself sharp with a good night's sleep. Unfortunately, anxiety kept him from all but three hours of sack time. His nervous system was vibrating off the charts. He just couldn't wait to see what his next assignment would bring.

He deboarded with his four friends from training—Bob Craig, Jeff Allen, Skip Green, and Herb Harrison. They had been assigned as a team of sorts to replace a group of comparable size. The car that brought their predecessors to the airport whisked Jamie and his team back to the US embassy. It was just a thirty-minute ride. After lunch, they were assigned to their rooms in a lower basement area of the sizeable structure. They were to be known to their host country as members of the State Department assigned to various administrative tasks. The king and his long list of relatives were not naive about such descriptions, but they knew how to play the game, and it all seemed to work out in everybody's favor. The afternoon of their arrival was to be their downtime. By the time they had hung their clothes, made their beds, and had a quick tour of the embassy, it was time for their welcome dinner.

Charles Crowley, the US ambassador—who preferred to be known as Chuck—gave a welcome speech in a special dining area within the embassy where he could talk openly about some of the secret functions Jamie and his comrades would be performing. The food was great, and the talk proved fascinating. Even with his previous background, Jamie couldn't believe the degree of devious behavior the US government required to deal with a supposed ally like Saudi Arabia. But that was just the beginning. This was much more than a base used to spy on the Saudis. It was the home of our extensive and incredibly intricate spy network in the Middle East. Jamie soon began to realize how incredibly important this mission of his team was to the safety of the United States.

After ten hours of solid sleep, Jamie, Bob, Jeff, Skip, and Herb sat down for a breakfast meeting where they discussed highlights from the previous night. They all seemed to be getting their bearings after realizing the enormity of their mission. During this discussion, Jamie seemed to emerge as the natural leader of the group. Although they were all at the same level within the CIA, his earlier experience with the army always seemed to make him the go-to guy.

Of all the assignments, the most difficult would be dealing with Iran. Not only was the recent hostage taking an issue of extreme delicacy, Iran, a largely Shiite country, was thoroughly unloved by the Saudis. When the time came to sort out the countries each member of the team would handle, Iran was dealt to Jamie. Bob was given Iraq, Jeff was dealt Pakistan, Skip would manage Afghanistan, and Herb received America's most important ally in the region, Israel. At midmorning, the five men were again brought to a sequestered meeting area deep in the bowels of the embassy. A few minutes later, a senior CIA official came in pushing a cart filled with five file boxes, one for each member of the group.

"Men, these are the files prepared by your predecessors here in Saudi. They're the initial step in your *advanced* training with the CIA. I'll expect you to take them back to your rooms and study them thoroughly for the next three days. You'll be expected to know the names of all the key players in your assigned country and have a working knowledge of the key issues going on there from the recent past to the present time. You will each be quizzed on this information and be expected to be conversant regarding both key people and political points. You will then be given an intense course in the primary language or languages in your assigned country. During this six-week session, you will be expected to spend 80 percent of your time on language, 15 percent on reading and rereading the content of these files, and 5 percent on updating all that is occurring on a daily basis. You'll each have your own administrative assistant to handle outgoing communications and to feed you updated information. Are there any questions?"

At first, there was a deadly silence as each of the five men stared openmouthed at the volumes of paper before them. Then Jamie raised his hand. "Sir, will we have access to the guys who preceded us if we have questions on their information or need interpretations of their opinions on what we find?"

"The answer to that is a decided maybe. Those men will be scattered around the world over the next few weeks and maybe inaccessible. However, if it's possible, we would certainly want you to get as much information as you can from them. Just read what you have and let me know if you have concerns. And for the record, I personally prefer a somewhat informal relationship with your group. So just can the 'sir' business. The formal name is Senior Agent Stuart Johnson, but let's just keep it at Stu. That's all."

Chapter Ten

Three days passed. One would have thought these five normally outgoing and often boisterous young men had been sound asleep. Each, however, was in his own world memorizing the unfamiliar names of sheikhs and kings, tribesmen and warlords, cultures and conflicts until it all began to swirl in their minds like a maze that was starving for a solution. Jamie finally ended up covering one wall in his room with cardboard panels and pinning pictures with names as captions to create what looked like a series of family trees that helped him recognize the players visually and associate them with their often difficult names. Beneath each name, he placed a pronunciation breakdown to be sure he would not offend anyone or give away his lack of knowledge and experience. It didn't take long for his buddies to observe this and follow suit.

After three days, the group met with Stu to demonstrate what they had learned. Stu opened the meeting. "Well, men, if you're like most, I suspect you're all a little overwhelmed by your first assignment." He turned to Herb and said, "In Israel, give me the names of the top six politicians in order of seniority, the name of the minister of defense, the most important general, and the names and dates of each war going back to 1948."

Herb smiled and casually rattled off the answers.

Stu responded, "Very good, Herb. You get an A. But of course, you also had the easiest assignment as we all know more about the Israelis than any of the other countries involved. So let me move along to your friends and see what they know."

As Stu heard the almost error-free responses, he smiled with delight and a bit of surprise. No other group had ever been so competent in their first challenge. Then came Jamie's turn. Iran was sure to be the most challenging because the United States had severed relations with the country after the hostage crisis. As he began to ask his questions, Stu noticed Jamie closed his eyes while answering and moved his head much as one would while reading.

"Tell me, Jamie, why do you close your eyes when you respond?"

"Well, Stu, it helps me to read the chart."

"The chart…what are you talking about?"

"Would you like to see it?" Jamie asked.

"I guess I would since I really don't know what you're talking about."

Jamie got up, and Stu followed him to his room. The rest of the men followed behind. When Stu saw Jamie's cardboard wall, it all seemed to make sense. But he wasn't completely sure. Before he could ask further, Jamie said, "I created this wall to help me memorize the key players and their names. I also have a photographic memory. It's just habit, I guess, as far as my eyes are concerned. Actually, I can see the wall in my mind's eye, which allows me to see all the answers any time I call them up. I could, of course, do it with my eyes open if you'd rather."

"Indeed, I would," said Stu, and Jamie complied.

As they returned to the test room, Stu noticed similar charts on the walls of each man's room.

"Who came up with this chart idea?" he asked.

"Jamie," said Herb.

"Great stuff," said Stu. "We'll have to make this concept part of our future instruction to newcomers. Congratulations, Jamie, on a terrific idea."

Chapter Eleven

Driving Emma home from their evening of karaoke and food in North Fork, Mo caught a happy glimpse of Emma starting to smile. Nothing could have warmed his heart more than to see the love of his life show just a bit of happiness. It was to be the first sign of Emma returning to her former self.

Mo continued seeing Emma on a regular basis. She would tell him about teaching and then about what she was hearing from Jamie. Most of what she heard was pretty general stuff because he couldn't tell her about his work beyond the fact that it was "interesting" and "exciting." While Emma yearned for more substance, this was all she could get. So Mo filled in the substantive part by telling her about his business, how it was growing, and ideas he had for the future. She seemed interested, but he often found her staring into the distance, likely wondering if her marriage would continue or simply melt away.

It went on like this for months until Emma received a telegram from Jamie that his first R&R would be coming up in four weeks. Because that would be at the beginning of September, he told Emma he would love to meet her in New York City and spend a week alone with her before coming back to Salmon. He thought seven days in a luxury hotel, eating at great restaurants, and seeing Broadway plays would be a fun way to reconnect.

Emma was thrilled and cautious at the same time. Visiting New York City would be great fun. But the thought of Jamie trying to convince her to live there in the future would ruin the whole experience. It was hard to tell her to go, but Mo knew it was the right thing. At some point, Emma had to make it with Jamie or come home to the man who couldn't live without her.

She went, and when she and Jamie returned to Salmon, she seemed ecstatic. They had had a great time in the city, and she later confessed to Mo that Jamie hadn't tried to sell her at all. Mo just had to let it go.

Chapter Twelve

Emma's time in New York was the worst time of Mo's life. *The nerve of Jamie*, he thought to himself. The intruding "stranger" trying to take the place of Emma's surrogate husband. The fact that he had spent more time with Emma since she and Jamie had been married had truly made him feel like the real husband in every way but one. *This*, he thought, *had to change*.

It seemed like forever until the day Mo drove Emma and Jamie to the airport. Their month together had obviously reawakened the warmth between them, but previous experience told Mo that with Jamie spending another full year away from home, Emma would be coming back to her "true love" soon.

She seemed a bit sad and noticeably quiet as they drove home. Mo didn't think breaking into her thoughts at that moment would be wise. He dropped her at home, gave her a brief hug and friendly kiss on the cheek, then left with nary a word.

Mo's dad had asked for a meeting at their office to discuss a matter about which he seemed terribly secretive. Mo drove straight there from Emma's, and when he arrived, his dad and Ali Hasson—his dad's friend from Iran—were there alone. When Mo entered, the heavy cloud of smoke in this dimly lit room told him they had been there for some time.

"Come in, my boy," said his dad. "Ali and I have an issue of grave importance to discuss with you."

It wasn't at all like his dad to be so serious about anything at that stage of his life. Mo was really running the company, and his dad had begun to adopt a fairly relaxed lifestyle. Now both he and Ali looked deadly serious.

His dad said, "Mohammed, there's something that you must now know. I've kept you from involvement in the last few years, but now it's necessary for you to be informed as the day could soon come when you must take over."

"Take over what?" Mo asked. "The two of you seem to suddenly have the weight of the world on your shoulders."

"In a way, it's true," said Ali. "But it's not quite the whole world, just our homeland, Iran. All of us were delighted to see the shah go. Now we have a state where our blessed Islamic faith leads the way. We have been heartened by this event, but our economy still suffers from growing restrictions imposed by the United States and other countries. Now the mullahs are asking all Iranians throughout the world to help the cause by donating money. We cannot do this openly here as US citizens are forbidden to aid the Iranian government. So your father and I have created a secret charity called IGO that supposedly supports the rehabilitation of wounded US military personnel. In reality, however, IGO is an abbreviation for Iranian Government Operatives. We actually do donate 25 percent to the US military veterans to create a true sense of legitimacy. The other 75 percent of the funds are laundered through a Canadian bank that transfers the money to the Iranian government through a shell company established in the homeland. This has been an ongoing project for a while now, but we need you to know all the intricacies and contacts. We see you heading up the operation in the next few years as we get older and may even pass on."

Mo was stunned. He had just left Jamie as he was going back to the Middle East to no doubt spy on their Islamic brethren, and suddenly he was being asked to join an illegal cabal supporting those very people. But it was his dad asking, and it was a calling from the country of his birth. "Dad," he said, "this, as you can imagine, comes to me as a total shock. You know I've always done your bidding as a son should do. But now you're asking me to defy the law of the country where I am now a citizen. Out of respect to your cause, I just—"

"*Stop*! Say nothing more, my son," his father interrupted. "This is not a request. This is an order! You will do this and do it without hesitation or regret. I too am a US citizen, but I am a proud Shiite Muslim from Iran, and that is where my and your first and last loyalty must always be placed. Do I make myself clear?"

Mo's father had never yelled at him before. He always had a soft and rational way about him and had gained Mo's love and respect. To hear his voice raised to this pitch made Mo step back. He stood in silent shock for a few moments.

"Father," he finally said, "you have never spoken to me in this tone before. Obviously, this is a matter of extraordinary importance to you. I will, of course, bend to your wish. Please provide me with the details and ultimate goals of IGO, and I will do everything I can to bring success to its cause."

Chapter Thirteen

Jamie returned to the Saudi embassy after rehashing his four weeks with Emma over and over on the plane ride. He felt sure the fences that were so in need of mending were back in repair and that the idea of divorce had been flushed from Emma's mind. He could again concentrate on the harrowing nature of his work with a clear head. Funny, he thought to himself, how he had come to inherit Iran as his assignment. He probably could have learned a lot from Mohammed, of all people, if only he had the freedom to discuss his assignment with him.

He still had twenty-four hours to adjust to the time zone and shoot the breeze with his buddies before things got serious. The five of them quickly put their gear away and went to the in-house bar for a few cool ones. The next few hours were nonstop chatter as everyone relived their time stateside. Then it was off to bed for an early start on a whole new life for each of them.

Herb was the lucky one. He was on a secured flight to Israel before the others were up. Even though he would be doing some spying on the United States' closest ally, it was an ally, and even when he was in-country, he would be on pretty safe turf. As long as he got along with the Mossad (instead of being caught by them), he would be okay.

In short order, Jeff was called away from breakfast. He said goodbye to his pals and was soon on his way to a safe house in Lahore, Pakistan. In another thirty minutes, Skip found himself bound for Kabul, Afghanistan. Finally, Bob was called aside and in short order was off to Bagdad, leaving Jamie alone, savoring his last bit of coffee.

Stu appeared. "Jamie," he said as he sidled up to the breakfast table and took a seat. "Now that your friends have departed, I thought it best that we have a special and very critical discussion about your assignment in Iran. As you know, we asked all of you except Herb to start growing full beards shortly after you arrived in Riyadh. Obviously, this is to help you be well accepted in Muslim countries. While all of you, except Herb, have new names appropriate to your new country of origin, *your* level of potential danger will be much greater. It will be especially important that you always use your new name Assaf Mohammed. It will be of particular importance to you because once you leave this place, you will no longer be you!"

Jamie's face was puzzled.

Stu continued, "As we have no relationship at this time with Iran, you will always be referred to as Assaf Mohammed."

"For as long as you are on this assignment, Jamie Duncan will be a name in cold storage everywhere. That means that all contacts with the CIA will be with your new name. You will also be unable to communicate with anyone in the States, including your wife, unless you are here in the embassy for briefings or other business reasons. We will advise your wife of this situation so that she understands the circumstances and will not be concerned by your lack of communication."

Jamie nodded slowly, and Stu continued, "Getting back briefly to the beard, it will be critical to your safety. You will be working from several secret locations…safe houses. You will rotate between these locations for varying lengths of time, of which you will be advised by coded messages. Each of these safe houses will be fully equipped with food, clothing, and special communications equipment you will need to relay information to us here at the embassy. It will be critical to your safety that you follow the schedules we provide in moving between these locations. Again, all communications will be encoded, and the codes will be changed once each month. You know all the codes from your training. Each code system will be identified by simple numbers—ten, twenty-five, fifty, or seventy-five."

As Jamie nodded his understanding, Stu went on. "Unlike your friends, it will not be possible for you to fly into Tehran. However, we do have a handful of 'assets' in-country that we have developed and trust, who will meet you tonight at the border in a desert area. They will drive you on a back road to a location just a mile or so from a major highway leading to Tehran. We have another man you will meet there who will take you into the city and your first home away from home. When you arrive there, you will use this combination that I am giving you to open the safe you will find hidden under the floorboards directly in front of the oven. The instructions for your first assignment in-country will be found there. I would give them to you now, but we can't risk your being captured with that information on your person. It would mean a certain death sentence!"

This was a bit more than Jamie was expecting. For the first time in his life, he began to know the true meaning of the word *fear*.

"Jamie, be ready to leave at 1100 hours. You'll first be driven to a rural area on the Persian Gulf. There, you will cross the Gulf in a high-speed boat accompanied by a contingent of Navy SEALs. About a half mile from shore, the SEALs will move with you into an inflatable, which they will paddle to the coastline. The Iranian asset will meet you there, and you'll be on your way. Good luck, young man! We're really counting on you for some critical information. Stay safe!"

Jamie and Stu shook hands before Stu walked out, leaving Jamie with his thoughts of what was to come. A whole range of emotions—excitement, fear, anxiety—spun through his mind like a tornado. Finally, he was on his way. He thought about how far he had come since the day he had heard from Jay Collins about the CIA. He thought then of Emma and hoped the lack of communication would not cause another major problem.

Chapter Fourteen

Emma, of course, knew Jamie was not allowed to communicate, but she was concerned for his safety. She didn't know where he was. He could still be at the US embassy in Saudi Arabia or anywhere else in the Middle East. However, as time dragged on, she began to again feel a distance growing between them. She was calling Mo almost every day. The more she talked, the more he was able to form a true picture of what was going on in her mind. It wasn't a picture that favored her absentee husband. Another month passed and then another. She came to Mo one evening as he was closing his store in Salmon.

"Mohammed, I think I need a drink. I can't take this anymore. Please come with me to North Fork. I have to clear my mind…or maybe cloud it. This life I'm leading is just a disaster."

Mo had been listening to this kind of complaint for some time now, and while Emma's frustrations had been building, his were right there with hers. He decided it was time to make his move. Emma and Jamie's marriage had become a farce.

Emma had never been much of a drinker, just a beer here and there to be part of the crowd. But that evening, she decided to start with a martini—the first one she had ever had. It was icy cold, and with her first sip, Emma scrunched up her nose as its power overcame her system. Yet she plowed on, finishing the first one and asking Mo to order a second. With each sip, her body began to adapt, and her mouth ran on with breathtaking speed, spilling out, it seemed, every negative thought she had ever had about her marriage. Mo listened, nodded calmly in concurrence, and watched her play herself into his silent web. He had to admit feeling a traitor to Jamie and, in a way, to Emma, but in his heart, he knew that bringing her to him at long last would be best for all of them. He would finally have the woman he had always wanted. Jamie would be free to roam the world with his adventurous new career, and Emma would have a husband who adored her and would love living in Salmon with her for the rest of their lives. It was a perfect scenario.

They had arrived in North Fork at 6:00 p.m. It was now 9:00 p.m., and Emma was doing her best to finish her fourth martini. Mo could see her eyelids beginning to sag and listened as her speech began to slur. She had let go of all the sadness that had been building up inside and now found herself leaning on Mo's shoulder, her hand unconsciously on his upper thigh. Her touch, innocent as it was, drove him crazy. He'd wanted her from the first moment he had seen her as a high school freshman. Now years later, that desire had grown to an overwhelming passion that was triggered even by this slightest touch.

"Emma," he said, "I think you've probably had all the liquor you can handle. What say I take you home?'

She slowly responded, "Okay, Mo, I guess I'm ready, but please don't leave me there alone. I just need you with me. Please!"

"You know I would never leave you, that I've always been here for you. You're my best friend, Em, and I love you dearly."

"Thanks, honey," she replied as she tried to rise from the barstool. Thankfully, Mo was able to catch her before she stumbled. He guided her to the car, got her seated, and started back to Salmon. Emma was sound asleep in a minute and stayed that way until they arrived at her front door. Mo came around to her side and tried to wake her, without success. He then managed to turn her in the seat to a point where he could cradle her in his arms, carry her into her house, and lay her down in bed. He looked at her deep in sleep, so beautiful just to watch. Then Mo took a chance. He leaned over close to her and kissed her softly on the lips. She stirred slightly and smiled but didn't wake. Finally, he had kissed those perfect lips, and it sent a thrill down his spine.

It was 3:00 a.m. when Emma finally stirred. She blinked her eyes a few times as she lay in the dark wondering for a moment where she was. As her vision cleared, she saw familiar surroundings and wondered how she had gotten there. She was under the covers but sleeping in just her underwear, something she never did. She sat up and turned on the light. On the chair next to her bed were her skirt and sweater, neatly folded. Her shoes were next to the chair. Her head was throbbing.

Finally, everything started to come back: The stop at North Fork with Mohammed. The martinis. A vague memory of her getting into the car. Then it was blank. Obviously, Mo had brought her home and put her to bed. Her face began to redden at the thought of him seeing her the way she now was. *Then again*, she thought, *he's really become my very best friend and someone I've really grown to care for and depend on. After all, I would do the same for him if the situation were reversed and not think anything of it.*

She lay back again and doused the light. All the thoughts she had been having the previous day about Jamie and her life situation came roaring back. She closed her eyes and let everything run through her mind two, three, four times. And then came a new thought, this time of Mohammed. What an anchor he had been, holding her together whenever she had troubles.

Always kind, incredibly gentle, and understanding. She thought, *Here is a man I've known nearly half my life with all the traits I've always wanted and admired in a man, and I've been so blind to it all. I've always fallen for Jamie's good looks, intelligence, and outgoing personality while Mo's soft and reticent demeanor was hiding the traits I've always valued most. Have I made a grave error? Have I been a fool? Has my love been misplaced all these years?*

Emma sat up and again turned on the light. She rubbed her eyes to be sure she was fully awake and again checked the clock. It was 3:30 a.m., and suddenly, she found herself beginning to form a whole new outlook on her life. It was a stunning and life-altering moment.

Chapter Fifteen

Jamie's ride through the desert to the Persian Gulf proved uneventful. When he met the four navy SEALs, however, his heart began to pump at a new rate. These studs, all dressed in battle gear and camouflaged for the occasion, brought a new level of excitement to his mission. The first thing they did to Jamie was to cover his white robe with the proper uniform for the trip and to put a bit of facial camouflage on the parts of his face not covered by his new beard. They also gave him a special gel that would remove the cammo after he was in the first car.

The preparation didn't take long. Not much talk, just fast action! Jamie was just beginning to find himself comfortable in his new element as they hustled him into the speedboat for their run across the Gulf. At fifty knots on calm seas, this incredibly swift craft would cross the water in just four hours. About a half mile from shore and about twenty miles north of Bushehr, the boat stopped. Two of the SEALs off-loaded an inflatable raft, which was quickly filled with air. One man boarded the raft while the other handed Jamie two sets of oars. Jamie was next in, followed by the second SEAL. They rode quickly and quietly to shore. As they reached a small cove along the shoreline, they used a flashlight to signal to the CIA's Iranian agent,

Ashraf, who promptly returned the light signal and emerged from a forested area.

Introductions were fast as the SEALS wished Jamie well and quickly reboarded the raft for the trip back to their boat.

Ashraf motioned for Jamie to come quickly with him into the woods. They followed a narrow path through a heavily forested area for a few hundred yards until they came upon a small opening. In this small glen sat an old Land Rover painted black but in serious need of washing. The side and rear windows were tinted black. Ashraf motioned for Jamie to hop in the front passenger seat while he entered and took the wheel. Once in, Ashraf began to speak in English but with a very heavy accent, referring to Jamie by his newly assumed name, Assaf.

"Assaf, I am happy you have had a good trip 'til now. Unfortunately, the hard part is to come. I have made this trip twice before without incident, but it is definitely risky. I have been told to give you two items for the journey that I hope you will never need."

With that, Ashraf handed Jamie a loaded pistol with a silencer attached and a small plastic envelope. In it was a white pill.

"Assaf, these are obviously for your protection. You know how to use the pistol, and the silencer is to keep you from drawing attention to yourself should there be a problem. The pill is in case all else fails. You do not want to be captured under any circumstances by the Republican Guard!"

Jamie swallowed hard as Ashraf urged the car forward onto a narrow dirt road that would lead them to a two-lane highway that would take them into Tehran. Once on the road, Ashraf explained that it would be about an eight-hour journey to the meeting point with Jamie's second contact. The car he would see there would look very different from the one they were in and would be found in a long-abandoned industrial park about a mile outside Tehran. While in good working order, it would be very old and tired to blend in with the cars on the streets in Tehran.

The man in that car would be known as Kareem. He would get Jamie to his final destination.

Now settled in and with a bit more specific knowledge of what was ahead, Jamie gazed across the partly mountainous, but mostly desertlike landscape looking for, but hoping never to find, roaming patrols of the Iranian guard. He estimated the arrival at the meeting point to be about 7:00 p.m. Ashraf had brought water and some falafel sandwiches for the trip. That way, the only stops would be for toilet breaks and fuel.

At 6:30 Jamie could see vague outlines of the Tehran skyline. The winds were up, causing sand to fly and reduce visibility. They also began to encounter light traffic that slowed their pace. Suddenly, Ashraf pulled off onto a small side road.

"We're getting close," said Ashraf. "I expect we'll be there in another ten minutes. Keep the pistol handy. You never know what to expect out here."

Jamie felt his heart suddenly pounding at an accelerated rate. He felt his hand beginning to sweat as he grabbed the handle of the gun. The sun was now low in the sky, and the winds began to calm as quickly as they had risen. The car made a sharp turn and suddenly the old industrial area was in front of them. Ashraf slowed the car and cautiously approached a large one-story building that looked like an old warehouse. One of the overhead doors in the back had been left open. In the loading dock was an old green Toyota sedan. No one, however, seemed to be around.

"Be careful here, Assaf. On my previous trips here, Kareem was always in the car and would flash his lights one time to acknowledge my arrival. Obviously, that's not happening. We'll park around the corner of the building so we aren't exposed, just in case there's a trap."

The two men left the Land Rover with guns drawn. They were able to keep a low profile behind a small concrete stairway until they were within a few feet of the open door. As they moved closer, they could hear someone moaning. Ashraf motioned to Jamie to hold still as he rushed ahead. Suddenly, shots rang out. Two soldiers with automatic weapons appeared from behind a wall at the back of the dock area and began to fire at Ashraf. Jamie, an expert marksman from his army days, was unseen and had a clear shot. He quickly drew his pistol, took aim, and fired. He dropped the first man with a perfect shot to the chest. The second man then saw Jamie and moved to fire back. That was Ashraf s chance as he took him out before he could fire. Jamie then ran forward as they checked to be sure both men were dead. When one moved, Jamie did a double tap to the head of each of them to be sure the excitement was over.

While Jamie was pulling the bodies out of sight, Ashraf checked on Kareem in the car.

The moaning had stopped. His friend had bled out.

"We must go now," said Ashraf. "I'm going to leave Kareem in his car and close the door. The Iranian guard must have been suspicious of him for some reason. I don't want us to travel in that car. We'll stick with the Land Rover and get you home as quickly as possible."

Chapter Sixteen

Months passed. Jamie was back at his first safe house. The routine of moving locations and dodging the Iranian version of the CIA, along with the Republican Guard, was becoming routine, if you consider living in constant fear for your life routine.

Working with only two Iranian assets, whom he fully trusted, along with a member of the Mossad that he now had occasion to work with on a joint project with Israel, Jamie had begun to put together a more complete and better-defined picture of what the United States was facing in its arm's length relationship with Iran. The real problem, however, was getting an insider's position and view. No one, not even the local assets, were close enough to the mullahs to know their full intentions. For Jamie to be in that position himself would be virtually impossible. The trick, if he were to make his mission a real success, would be to convert a high-level insider to the United States cause. No small trick.

Jamie decided that now, six months into his stay, with his language skills well-developed and the lay of the land clear, he had to find the right man to turn. There were two, both of whom would be considered outside possibilities at best. He had a slight preference for one of them, Samir

Allem, whom he had met in a sales meeting under his guise as a local food merchant. This man had purchased a large quantity of dates for his sizeable wholesale food company. The two of them had hit it off personally and after several months began to develop a real friendship.

Samir one day asked Jamie (whom he knew as Assaf) to dinner with his family. This, Jamie knew, could be the break he had been waiting for.

It was 5:00 p.m. when the taxi arrived at the palatial home of his new friend and customer.

He pulled a cord at the entrance. A servant came from inside and unlatched the gate, then motioned silently for Jamie to follow him.

As he entered the house, Jamie found it hard to believe the apparent wealth of this otherwise unpretentious man he was now calling "friend." The man who led him into the house then asked him to wait in the sumptuous sky-lighted foyer. As soon as he left, a veiled woman appeared. Even beneath her flowing robes, Jamie sensed a woman of extraordinary beauty.

"I am Soya Allem," she stated softly. "My husband speaks very highly of you, Assaf. May I say that I appreciate your new friendship with him. He works constantly and never seems to have time for social friendships. I know his relationship with you will be good for him."

"Well, your husband has said he was fortunate to have been given such a wonderful wife in an arranged marriage. Few, he said, are as fortunate as him."

"That is always wonderful to hear," she responded. Without another word, she motioned for Jamie to follow

54

her to the grand hall. As they entered the room, he spotted Samir seated on a large couch with three young children beside him.

"Welcome, my friend," he said, as he rose with a warm smile on his face. "You have met my wonderful wife, Soya. Please meet our three children, Yussef, Kareem, and Abdullah."

The children clung closely to their father, forced smiles, and offered a mild "Assalamu alaikum."

Jamie responded in kind. As he did so, a small parade of servants entered with plates filled with fruits and local specialties appetizers to what he suspected would be a true representation of the word *feast*. He was quite right.

Chapter Seventeen

After her drunken stupor, Emma had been in and out of bed, first pacing, then on her back staring at the ceiling, then back on her feet again unable to sleep. At 6:00 a.m., she gave up on the idea of rest and took to the shower. The rushing water helped sober and refine her thoughts about life. She thought, *It's time to have a talk with Mohammed.*

Mo always worked at his original shop in Salmon on Mondays. They opened at 7:00 a.m., and Mo was unlocking the door when Emma arrived carrying coffee and his favorite doughnut from the local bakery.

Mo was stunned when he saw her arrive at that early hour. Her face exhibited an unusually bright smile, the kind she used to have all the time but had seldom had since the loss of her baby.

"Thanks, Mo," she said, "for everything yesterday. I must have been quite a sight after North Fork. Only you could have gotten me through all the twists and turns of yesterday. The very least I can do is offer you this 'waker-upper.'"

She put down the treats and, without another word, took his slack-jawed face in her hands and kissed him full on the lips. He instinctively closed his eyes and then opened them, looking directly into hers. Then he stepped close to her, enveloped her in his arms, and kissed her back—a long, slow, warm kiss that brought more than just their lips together. He continued to hug her, never wanting to let go of this moment he had dreamed of for years.

With her arms still around his neck, she whispered, "Mo, I woke up at 3:00 this morning sorting out thoughts that I had been having not just about Jamie but about you and me and our incredible friendship. Finally, I came to realize how you've become the most important person in my life. With every situation I've encountered since my miscarriage, you've been the major player in setting me right. It's as though you're my husband without being so. When I stepped out of the shower this morning, I felt as though you should have been there to hold me…and love me."

Mo stood there holding her, now in a total state of shock. The love he had been harboring for her for all these years, it seemed, now had a right to flow out and surround them both with great joy. He did his best to gather himself and separate their bodies enough to look straight into her beautiful eyes.

"Em," he said with a quiver in his voice, "I owe you a long-overdue explanation. On our very first day of high school, the day when Jamie and I watched you walk into and light up the room, I fell in love with you. Neither of us knew you, but both of us were dumbstruck. The difference was that my quiet personality kept me from speaking up while Jamie captured your attention and, later, your love. Now the time has shown you that first impressions are not always lasting. I've always held back from saying or doing anything that would damage your marriage or destroy my friendship with Jamie. But secretly I had hoped for a moment like this when you would see me as the man who has loved you for all these years and that you would be the one to say it first. Now, finally, my lifelong dream has come true."

At that moment, Mo's coworker Katrina, who usually handled the counter, entered. He quickly separated his hold on Emma and pretended that it had been a playful platonic hug.

Fortunately, Emma did have some cleaning to pick up and handed Mo her claim check in a businesslike manner. He retrieved her items, and she casually paid, all under Katrina's watchful eyes.

It was Saturday, so without a classroom to go to, Mo knew Emma was likely to return home to do her weekend chores. He left the shop at noon as he normally did on weekends, but instead of heading to the diner for lunch, he headed to Emma's to continue their conversation. He found her in the backyard hanging her wash on the clothesline (some habits do die hard in rural Idaho). He was out of sight as he observed her finish with her wash line and return indoors. He then walked to the back door and knocked. When she saw who it was, she motioned him to come inside. The door closed behind him, and Emma came close. He felt her warmth and saw that smile reappear in all its brilliance before she embraced him and then tilted her head back so he could kiss her again. Without another word, they both knew what they wanted next and walked toward her bedroom.

As they slipped out of their clothes, Emma stopped for a moment and said, "When you brought me home yesterday, you partially undressed me before putting me under the covers. I think I'd like it if you finish the job now."

He was down to his boxer shorts, and she was the way he had left her the day before in bra and panties. He felt his heart racing, and his breath shorten as he removed her bra, seeing her perfect breasts for the first time. He hesitated for a moment and then slipped her panties to the floor. She casually stepped free of them and then close to him. Then without a word, she removed his shorts and saw all of him.

How does one express the feelings he had at that moment? So much love, such erotic excitement, the revealing of this body so long admired and desired. He felt nailed to the floor, not knowing what to do next, but Em, in her incredible way, sensed his unease and casually touched him in his most sensitive place.

"Come lie down with me, my love," she whispered. "It's time we knew each other in the one way we've never explored."

As they held each other in bed, touching all those places that had previously been unavailable, kissing and holding each other and enjoying the warmth of their bodies and emotions, he finally entered her and experienced her warmth around him in the way that makes a man and woman as close as they can possibly be. It was this moment and the climax that soon followed that brought him to a state of absolute euphoria.

Chapter Eighteen

Dessert was winding down. Soya quietly moved the three boys from the table, coaching them to say goodbye to their guest and kiss their father before retiring. The long dinner and the unusual (in these parts) consumption of fine wines had put Samir in a relaxed and talkative mood. While the use of alcohol was not accepted practice among the populace, the elites, if only in the privacy of their own homes, would engage, especially if they tended to be more secular than observers of strict Sharia law.

Jamie had tempered his drinking during dinner to be sure his head was clear for this important opportunity to strike. In previous conversations with Samir, he had gauged a sense of frustration with the strictness placed on Iranian society by the mullahs. He could tell Samir truly wished for a more liberal and preferably democratic approach to government. Now in this environment, Samir felt an opening had been created.

"Tell me, Assaf, what do you think of our government and its leadership? What I mean is, do you prefer things as they are, or would you change anything if given the choice?" Samir asked.

Jamie intentionally paused a minute before answering what could be a dangerous question. Here, he knew that the wrong answer could raise a red flag while the right one could be the first step in turning Samir into the most significant US asset in Iran. For a long time, he had an overriding concern that had been with him since the beginning of his training at the Saudi embassy. He was a white man. He was not a natural speaker of the language. Could he really pass himself off as a born and bred Iranian? Wouldn't a man like Samir notice a strange accent or an unusual skin tone? Even with his full beard and suntan, would he be as carefully cloaked as he needed to be to pull this off? So far, things seemed fine. Neither Samir nor any of the other Iranians had questioned his nationality. He kept his fingers crossed and hoped his knack for adapting to local pronunciations was on target and that his vocabulary had become sufficiently expansive to handle the job.

He finally said, "I guess there isn't a perfect society anywhere in the world. However, I find that while a theocracy such as ours can have its positive side, I have never regarded Islam as a religion that professed evil as its core value. Unfortunately, at times, cruelty and repression seem to reign in the name of Islam. I find this to be an unfortunate application of what Allah would want. I think we can find ways to improve on the way things are handled today."

There was a long pause as quiet filled the room. Jamie watched Samir's facial expressions carefully as he awaited the words he anticipated, judging by the contemplative expression on his friend's face.

Finally, Samir spoke, "My dear Assaf, we have now known each other for just a few short months. Somehow, however, I feel that I have known you longer, if not better, than many I have known all my life. I have succeeded in this society in great measure because of circumstance. Many of those I grew up with in privilege have become the political strongmen of this country. All of them, save one, still operate at the pleasure of the mullahs. The one exception is one of the mullahs. Were the others allowed to be independent men, our world, and our relationship with other countries of the world would be far different today. What's more, the key person who keeps them among the elite was a childhood friend of our clique. He was the only one with a strict religious bent. Fortunately, he has always kept a warm spot in his heart for his childhood friends. Without his influence, this country could become an even darker place."

"I see," said Jamie. "That is quite an interesting background you came from, my friend. Your insights into how this country operates must indeed be deep, as youthful connections to people are usually the strongest. Those who knew you during your formative years are typically those who are most trusting of you and most loyal to you. I am glad that your outlook on government is what it is, but wouldn't it be wonderful if you could use your connections in a positive way? While you seem to feel that your secular friends would direct things in a more open fashion, they are hemmed in by the mullahs. But is there a chance that you as an individual, or your group of friends, could talk to your special mullah, who has a true power position, about making the lives of everyday Iranians more open and about opening up our society to the world at large?"

Now responding more quickly, Samir said, "If only your wishes could be made true, Assaf, this country would leap ahead. We have the brains, and our youth has the will-power. The trouble is that if even a hint of a rebellious word is spoken aloud—yes, even among my close friends—the result could mean death. No discussion. No trial. The traitor would simply disappear forever. Often, the immediate family would join him on this road to nowhere. We, all of us, live in constant fear of the whim of some religious zealot."

"Samir, I feel and share your pain. And while I am not close to those who control everything, I have long felt inclined to find a way to change our country. I know it can be frightening, especially for someone like yourself with a beautiful and happy family, and perhaps not worth the risk when you know you can live a full and even luxurious life by leaving things alone. However, I sense that you, like me, are not a man to sit back and let your country continue as an ongoing nemesis to itself and the world without trying to do something positive. I have a sincere feeling that this is why we have connected as we have, in friendship, as we both know there is a better way for all Iranians."

Jamie looked into his friend's eyes as Samir again contemplated his response. Suddenly, he rose from his chair and began to pace the room. It seemed as though he was totally alone with thoughts of many things he had considered over the years racing through his mind.

Finally, he walked toward Jamie, stopped in front of his new friend, and extended his arms toward him. Jamie stood, and the men embraced. When they separated, tears could be seen on Samir's face. It was as though a dam had been opened, and now the emotions began to flow. Finally, the ideas Samir had been considering for years seemed somehow to have a glimmer of hope.

"Assaf, it is getting late, and I have an exceptionally busy day ahead of me. I must think further of all we have discussed this evening. I promise you that when I have had a chance to lay things out in an orderly fashion, I will be in touch with you. Just give me a few weeks to get organized."

Jamie's taxi arrived in short order, and they bid farewell. As he rode back to his safe house, Jamie sensed that he was on the precipice of something great. If he was wrong… well, he didn't want to think about that!

Chapter Nineteen

The sun rose on Sunday morning. Mohammed awoke with his true love sleeping by his side. He couldn't take his eyes off the beautiful face looking so content just inches away. He must have lain there for half an hour just enjoying the view before Emma stirred and blinked her eyes. As she awoke, she looked at him, smiled, and placed her head on his shoulder. Their bodies melded with pure joy in the feeling of warmth they shared.

"Mo," she whispered, "I haven't felt this happy in ages. I don't know that I have ever felt so wanted, so loved. I really have to apologize for my being so blind all these years."

Mo just took in the words, felt the warmth, and allowed his personal nirvana to wash over him and grant him the joy he had yearned for, seemingly forever. Neither of them wanted to move, so they held each other, made love again, and finally gave in to the clock at noon to shower and engage the day.

Needless to say, Mo had to be careful about leaving the house. He loved this town, but like most small towns, word traveled fast, and everyone knew that Emma and Jamie were married. In addition, all their parents—Jamie's, Emma's, and Mo's—lived within a few blocks of where they were. They decided he would be better off waiting until nightfall before leaving, and in the future, they could arrange to be together in places that would be less suspect.

It wasn't until 10:00 p.m. that Mo left Emma's place, having just spent the happiest twenty-four hours of his life. He felt like skipping down the street like a child but had to be careful no one he knew would see him and ask questions. He made it home safely, went directly to his bedroom, and lay on his back. Staring at the ceiling, he recounted over and over again what had just happened so it would forever be emblazoned in his mind. Somewhere along the way, he fell into a deep and joyful sleep.

Chapter Twenty

Two long weeks passed before Jamie heard from Samir. Under the guise of a business call, Samir said, "Assaf, I am in serious need of some dates and want to discuss my order along with some new items I'm considering carrying in inventory." He listed the items and then said, "I'm just a bit under the weather today, so I'm working from home. Do you think you could come here and bring the samples with you?"

Samir's voice seemed to have an anxious tone to it, leading Jamie to suspect there was something much more important to this call than another order. He responded, "Of course, Samir. Let me put a few things together for you. I should be there in about an hour."

Jamie went through all the motions of gathering several samples of foodstuffs, taking his order book, packing his briefcase, and then hailing a taxi. He was at Samir's front gate in just forty-five minutes. He was let in by the same man he had met when he came for dinner. Once inside, Soya, looking a bit tense, welcomed him and led him to another part of the house—an underground office accessed through a hidden tunnel.

She patted his shoulder and whispered, "May Allah be with you both." Then she was gone.

Samir sat at the rear of this rather large room with his back to Jamie. He was whispering into his phone. In a moment, he concluded the call and spun around in his chair.

"Sit, my friend," he said with a serious look on his face. "I was talking with another friend just now, Ibrahim Ali, who is of like mind with us. We grew up together and share the same values and ideas for the future. He was the only person I spoke to about our conversation at dinner two weeks ago. He is most anxious to meet you. Oh, and by the way, I have plenty of dates in inventory. I just didn't want to take a chance that our government would be listening in on our call."

Ten minutes later, Ibrahim entered the room. Samir warmly embraced him and then formally introduced him to Jamie. "This is the young man I told you about, Ibrahim. I wanted you to meet another who shares our dream of a reconstructed Iran. Somehow, I think, we can find a way together to change the tide here."

Samir walked back to the rear of the office to be absolutely sure no one was on the other side of the door listening to their conversation. When he was sure of their safety, he returned and sat with Jamie and Ibrahim to lay out his ideas. Ibrahim followed with comments that were largely a reiteration of what Samir had to say. Jamie could tell that the two of them had been bandying these ideas about for a long time—probably years—without taking action. Now with him as the third member of this newly formed cabal, they seemed to be ready for that action. He knew this was the chance he had been waiting for.

Chapter Twenty-One

The next morning, Jamie paced the floor and wondered just how he was going to approach his new friends with the idea of partnership with the Great Satan to achieve their goals. He was hoping to be able to talk to his embassy contacts, but it turned out they were back in the States and out of touch "under any circumstances" for the next week. In his gut, he felt this chance couldn't wait that long. He sensed it had taken all Samir and Ibrahim's nerve to take their thoughts to him and that they might pull back without his giving them an immediate sense of direction.

He thought, *How can I tell them that I am an American without putting them in a state of shock and putting myself in mortal danger? On the one hand, they may see death coming from the mullahs, not only for themselves but for their families. Conversely, the idea of an overthrow of this crazy theocratic government would likely take the strength of a country like the United States, probably only the United States, to make change a reality.*

He searched for the words and approach that would ease them into the right thought process. He even rehearsed the conversation with himself, playing all three parts. After two days of intense planning and role-playing, he was ready to take his chances. He called Samir and arranged an appointment the following evening at Samir's home. He then lay down, mentally exhausted. As he tried to relax, his mind suddenly went back to Emma. Since coming to Iran, he realized that with all the stress he was under, there had been no thought of her for months. It was as though she had done much more than disappear from his everyday life; she had actually left his thoughts. *My god*, he thought to himself, *I know I've become Assaf to everyone here, but I really am still Jamie Duncan, American and husband to the love of my life. They always told me in training that stress had to be managed, but I guess it's taken over my life...or at least my personal life.*

It was a difficult night. He awoke several times with thoughts of Emma and then what was coming the next evening. When morning came, he knew he would need a full pot of coffee to keep himself awake as his mind focused on the difficult steps he'd be taking with this political dance of brinkmanship.

Chapter Twenty-Two

The weeks following their first night together were the happiest of Mo's life. Aside from the tension involved in sneaking away to a nearby town whenever they could, their love had grown exponentially. The realization of how right their relationship had become made both Emma and Mo feel like little kids again. All the parents involved (including Jamie's) commented on how happy they had both suddenly become even though they could see no apparent reason for their joy. This was one secret they knew others could never know, even if Jamie and Emma were to divorce. Without knowing it, Jamie and Mo were each engaged in their own sort of tap dance at the same time—each with the potential danger of being found out.

One night, as Emma and Mo were holding each other in the motel they had found a discreet distance from Salmon, they talked about their future and what they would do when Jamie returned. Emma seemed sure divorce was the only answer. The only question would be when to tell Jamie and how much to tell. Revealing their affair would, of course, be out of the question. Simply repeating her earlier comments about not being together as a basis for calling it off seemed to be the best answer. Then, after a waiting period during which Emma felt sure Jamie would move from Salmon and either stay with the CIA or end up on Wall Street, they could start to date publicly before finally marrying.

Chapter Twenty-Three

It was just after sundown when Jamie again arrived again at Samir's home. Once more, Soya ushered him into the underground office. Samir and Ibrahim awaited his arrival and looked at him with great expectation in their eyes.

"Welcome, my friend," said Samir. "Please sit with us. We are most interested in hearing what ideas you may have to get our 'revolution,' if you will, underway."

This was the moment. There was a brief and intentional silence before Jamie responded. Then he rose and began to speak as he paced the floor. He said, "I know that the two of you are lifelong friends and have absolute trust in each other. I have come into your lives and am a relative newcomer…yet you have spoken with me in good faith, knowing full well that if I were the wrong person, you and your families would be in mortal danger. I can't tell you how much I appreciate and respect your trust. No matter what, you can be sure I will always respect this trust and will never betray it."

Samir and Ibrahim looked at each other with curiosity as Jamie continued. "Because of what I have to say to you, I must ask that you listen to every word, no matter your immediate reaction, before responding. It is important that you see the full picture of what I am proposing before you respond. I say this because there are aspects of what I am about to tell you that will definitely put you in a state of shock and fill your minds with fear. That is why it is so important for you to have the complete picture."

Samir and Ibrahim looked at each other again, their expressions having changed from anticipation to wonderment and concern.

Jamie spoke again, "You have expressed both general direction and some specific changes that you would like to make in creating a new and secular Iranian government. You, as influential voices in this country, have also realized the extraordinary and, frankly, deadly difficulty presented in rising up against a government that is so tightly controlled and so evil to those who are perceived to have threatened its existence.

"Therefore, I must ask a rhetorical question from you. Do you think, with just three of us as the core group of rebels, that we, by ourselves—or even with a handful of others—could even make the slightest change in the status quo? *No!* It would be an impossible task. It will take much more in the way of espionage and likely military force to overcome the Republican Guard along with all the religious leaders. You will need help from a powerful source to even have a chance to make this work."

Jamie paused and then said, "I do have access to such a source. However, you will, I suspect, require a much-larger degree of trust in me to make this happen. I sincerely hope that you will have the necessary faith it will take to allow us to move ahead. Now, this minute, is where your faith in me and in your own ideas will be tested."

Jamie paused again and then shifted his gaze to look intently at the two seated men. "Gentlemen, tell me, what do you think when the leaders you both fear and despise refer to the Great Satan as your country's greatest enemy?"

The two men seemed to simultaneously jerk back in their chairs. They first looked at one another and then to Jamie. Samir finally stuttered, "Are you suggesting what I think you are suggesting? Because what I think you are suggesting is that we ally ourselves with what we have been told every day is the one country trying to destroy us."

"Wait, Samir. I know what your government thinks of the United States. I want to know what you think. And I want to know why," Jamie said.

Samir rose, and he too began to pace as he gathered his thoughts while Ibrahim squirmed in his seat, a quizzical look on his face. Finally, Samir spoke, "When the United States supported the shah, I hated them. They have made life so difficult for a number of Muslim countries. So I suppose it would be fair to say I was not crazy about the United States and its policies until I saw what we did, first at their embassy and then to ourselves with the outrageous behavior of the ayatollah and his regime. I suppose it would be fair to say that my negative perceptions of the United States have evolved, and I find myself longing more than you can imagine for the kind of freedoms US citizens enjoy every day. You should know that I did have the good fortune of spending a month there on a buying trip a number of years ago. The dynamics of the country made me want to stay longer just to soak it all in. However, Soya was with me and pregnant with our first child, so we did not have the luxury of time for all of that. Perhaps another time."

"Well," said Jamie, "now comes the moment of truth." He looked straight into Ibrahim's eyes and then at Samir. "I shall now give you the opportunity to stand up and be counted and perhaps to succeed in living out your dreams of seeing the rest of the USA."

"What?" asked the two men in concert. "We are not here to discuss vacations in the West!"

"Of course not. But it is the United States that is the one and only country with both the interest and capability of allowing you to realize your dreams of a new secular state. Remember, whatever we do to reorder the politics in this country, all three of us are going to be in constant danger. If that weren't true, we wouldn't be huddled in this underground office concerned that the wrong people might be listening. All of us are risking death. The only difference is that you are Iranians, and I am not!"

Ibrahim had never risen and watched dumbstruck as Samir fell backward into his desk chair, sending him rolling into the wall behind him. His heart was pounding. Ibrahim sat in stunned silence, his brown-skinned face paling in disbelief.

Jamie continued, "Now that I have told you my secret, please remember what I said when I began talking. Please listen to everything that I must say so you have the complete picture. I realize that you could pick up your phone, call the authorities, make up a plausible story, and have me arrested. I would then be thrown in prison, likely tortured, and finally hung if they could get no information from me or ransom for me. Keep that in mind in terms of what I said about all of us facing mortal danger. Remember too that I have the same goal as the two of you. The US government would much rather have Iran as an ally than an enemy."

Ibrahim suddenly rose and began, "But, Assaf, I must say…"

"Please don't," said Jamie. "It's important to let me finish. I'll certainly answer any questions you might have when I'm done." Ibrahim regained his seat, and Jamie continued, "As leaders of a new government, the two of you have the potential to be leaders for good, not only here in your country but as major players in the world. I know this is an incredible amount to absorb in a lifetime, let alone in a one-hour discussion, but this is reality, plain and simple. This kind of change requires daring and great risk. It's the only way to make happen what you have so long wanted to happen."

Samir stood, looked at Jamie, and said, "Would you please allow me to talk to my friend in private for a moment?" as he edged him toward the office door.

"Of course," said Jamie, as Samir closed the door behind him. He thought, *Well, this is it. They're either going to come out of there with guns blazing and bury me in the woods or with arms outstretched in friendship, willing to go all in and take the necessary chances.* He checked his watch. Ten minutes passed, then twenty more. Worry began to cast its shadow as Jamie paced back and forth in the short tunnel that led to the office. As he reached the far end of the tunnel, he turned back and again faced the office door.

At that moment, the door opened. The two white-robed men stood there looking him straight in the eye. Finally, it was Samir who spoke, "Assaf, we have been considering our chances. Not just the choice of life or death for ourselves, but the choice we are making for Soya, my three boys, and Ibrahim, his wife, Rama, and eleven children. We have agreed that we can risk our lives, but what are the chances that our families could be sent, at some point, to the States to save their lives? If we knew that could be done, we have agreed to go with you to the end. Tell us that this is possible."

"Gentlemen, I will never lie to you. Before I can make such a commitment, I must get permission. I won't be able to reach the necessary parties until next week. It may take a little while beyond that to get a final decision, but I will let you know as soon as I know. In the interim, I will work on plans for changing the government but think it best that we avoid unnecessary contact among us until I have an answer for you. And whatever you do, do not discuss our arrangement with anyone, including your wives, for everyone's safety."

The three men looked at one another and felt an unspoken sense of brotherhood. Then came a spontaneous embrace. Jamie felt success was almost at hand.

Chapter Twenty-Four

Stu Johnson, now back at the Saudi embassy, listened carefully as Jamie explained, over a secured phone, the details of his Iranian arrangement with Samir and his people. To say he was excited would be the grossest of understatements. It had seemed that ever since the takeover of the American embassy in 1979, the CIA had been plodding through glue in their efforts to make significant headway in Iran. To get two men with a high-end contact in the government and a deep-seated desire to initiate change to the status quo was like manna from heaven.

When he had heard everything, Stu said, "I will have to check with Langley about protecting the families, but my guess is they would agree to a protection plan much like the FBI gives to mobsters who testify against their own. Give me a couple of days, and I'll get back to you. In the meantime, I think you should make your first trip back to the embassy, where we can lay out a plan of attack that will feature Samir and Ibrahim as the point men."

"Sounds great to me," said Jamie. "Even though it's only Saudi, it will be a lot less stressful than being in Iran. Better food too. Can't wait!"

Three days later, Jamie made the perilous journey back to the embassy. He had the sensation that a weighted cloud was lifted from his shoulders. It was perhaps the first time he truly realized just how wonderful freedom felt. Empathy for those like Samir and Ibrahim overwhelmed him. Jamie Duncan, in his life as Assaf, was finally maturing in a meaningful way.

After a solid night's sleep, Jamie sat down with Stu and another CIA operative he had not previously met named Ken Griffin. Ken was there as a "listener." He had been fully briefed by Stu on what was happening in Iran and was to be kept up to date on every detail. It was also obvious that he was older, probably in his early forties, and quite experienced in espionage with the CIA. The three of them reviewed all the details to be sure they were on the same page. Then before Jamie could deliver what he thought might be the next move, Stu spoke up.

"Jamie, I can call you Jamie now because you will soon be relieved of your assignment in Iran. Ken will be replacing you. You will be making one final trip for the express purpose of introducing Ken to your new friends and convincing them that he is absolutely trustworthy and the most experienced man we have on all things Iranian. It is important first that you know everyone at Langley, not to mention yours truly feels that you have done an extraordinary job and shown brilliant initiative far beyond your age and experience level. It is also necessary that you understand that Ken has spent over ten years, off and on, working in Iran and has been the leader of a task force planning the next steps in our policy there after we got a breakthrough. You are the man who has provided that breakthrough. Now it's time for Ken to move in and for you to get a posh new assignment after a month on the home front with the wife who has been without you for the past year."

Jamie was dumbfounded. On the one hand, he wondered seriously how Samir and Ibrahim would react to this sudden and dramatic change. On the other hand, returning to Emma and being stateside for a month sounded like heaven. Then came the last part of Stu's epistle.

"Jamie, I thought you just might want to hear a little—just a little for now—about your new assignment."

"I'm all ears, boss. My fingers are all crossed, and I'm hoping for something very special," said Jamie.

"Oh, I think you'll feel good about this one," said Stu. "I suspect your wife will as well. I seem to remember you telling me that she's a first-grade teacher. Is that right?"

"Yes, sir, she is."

"Well, there just happens to be a very fine American school next to our embassy in Paris. And since that will be the site of your new office, the two of you could, at last, become next-door neighbors and reacquaint yourselves with each other."

"Paris! Oh my god. This is beyond my wildest dreams. Who do I have to thank for this?"

"Frankly, my good man, you have yourself to thank. It's the result of your exceptional work. Keep it up, and there's no telling where it might take you."

Three days later, Jamie and Ken (soon to be known as Ali) left for Iran. It was a duplication of Jamie's first trip to the country. After several close calls en route, they finally arrived at one of the safe houses. Jamie then reviewed his routine with Ken. Just hours after their arrival, a coded message came through that Langley would accept the members of Samir and Ibrahim's families if it was necessary to protect their safety. With this news, Jamie called Samir and set up an appointment for the following evening.

When he and Ken arrived at Samir's home, the man who had always led Jamie inside seemed surprised to find a second person—a stranger—in the company of Jamie. He asked that they both wait at the gate. He then ran back inside, and in a moment, Soya appeared with a distinctly worried look on her face.

"What is this?" she queried. "Samir expected you to be alone."

"The man you see here with me, Soya, is a key person in our meeting this evening. I will explain everything to Samir and Ibrahim in the office. Trust me, please, that everything is safe and secure."

Soya paused for a moment but then motioned for them to follow. She led them to the underground office, asked them to wait outside the door, and then entered and whispered a few words to Samir. He looked up at Jamie and the stranger with concern on his face, paused a moment, then motioned for them to enter. Soya left quietly, closing the door behind her.

The four of them sat, and Samir and Ibrahim waited for Jamie to explain. "Gentlemen," Jamie started, "I have two critical things to explain to you. After that, my associate, Ali, will go into far more detail of a plan designed to set all of us on a path for success in achieving our mutual goals."

He paused, then said, "First, the CIA has given approval of your request that in the event you feel the members of your families might be in peril, they will accept them into the United States, make provisions for hiding them, and provide them with passports, new names, safe homes, and an expedited path to citizenship. They will also assist in removing them safely from Iran. All you need to do to receive this assistance is advise Ali of the need, and he will set this plan in motion."

Jamie paused again, slightly dreading the next part of what he had to say. "The second thing is that I have been reassigned, much to my surprise, to a new position. While this was not my preference, I do not get a choice in matters like this. I have not been asked but *told* that the plan for my being here was just one year. No choice! Now let me tell you why, though we have become good friends, you will be happy that Ali is the man to relieve me."

Jamie then went on to detail Ali's extensive in-country experience, the fact that he had been developing a plan ever since the removal of the shah for the development of a secular and democratic government, exactly like the one the three of them had been hoping for. Before the evening ended (five hours and many toasts to success later), the confidence and trust that Jamie had built with these men had been effectively transferred to Ali. It was time for Jamie to make his way back to the States and the life he had left seemingly ages ago.

As he boarded the plane to go stateside, the words *separation* and *divorce*, which he had managed to force from his mind after coming to the Middle East, came surging up from his gut and made him wonder what it would be like to face Emma for the first time.

He had debated with himself whether he should let her know of his early release to R&R or if it should just be a surprise so that she didn't have time to prepare anything negative to say when he showed up at their front door. He decided on the latter.

Chapter Twenty-Five

Emma had just stepped out of the shower. It had been an unusually warm day in Salmon, and the school had no air-conditioning. She had just wrapped her hair in a towel and slung another towel around her torso when she was shocked to hear the front doorbell. She knew it wasn't Mo because he had planned a few days in the field to visit his satellite locations. Who could this possibly be at four in the afternoon?

She removed the towel, threw on a robe, and hurried to the front door. She pulled it open and then stood there, stunned. Before her stood a suntanned, newly shaved Jamie, sporting an army-style crew cut.

"Hi, Em," he said softly. "I was going to let you know but thought a surprise might be more fun. Can't tell you how great it feels to be home…how incredible it is to see my bride for the first time in ages, even more so because of the great news I have for us."

Emma stared, speechless. She couldn't move toward him yet didn't move away.

"Are you okay, Em? Aren't you even going to say hello or welcome me home or give me a hug?"

Emma continued to just stare, not knowing what to say. She was afraid to slip and say the wrong thing, yet she was not exhibiting the love one would expect from a wife who had not seen her husband for so long.

Finally, she took a step back and said, "Come in, Jamie. It's just that I'm in a state of shock. I couldn't imagine who would be showing up at my front door at four in the afternoon. You look well, all tanned and strong. You'll have to tell me all you can about your time in the Middle East or wherever it was that they ultimately sent you to spy on folks."

"Well, honey, we can get to all that. But somehow I get a sense of distance from you. You've always been the warmest, most inclusive person in the world, yet I suddenly feel cold. Like I'm being frozen out. What gives?"

She hesitated, then said, "I guess I would have liked to know you were coming. I had no basis for believing you would be back this soon, and I guess I just wasn't prepared. And without the ability for us to communicate, you had begun to slowly drop out of my everyday life. You must remember how we left things when you first went to Saudi Arabia. Things just don't change to perfection in a heartbeat. There has to be some time to reconnect. So please don't judge me too harshly. I just need some time to absorb what has just happened."

Jamie didn't know quite how to deal with her reaction but understood her position and didn't want to push too hard. "Okay, Em," he finally said. "I think I understand, but you should know that I am back with you now for good…or at least I hope so. I'm sure you'll remember my promise that if I didn't get the right kind of assignment, I'd leave the CIA. Well, my assignment in the Middle East has been ended in favor of another one that will be a dream job for both of us. Will you let me tell you about it?"

"Of course, Jamie, but I had just stepped out of the shower when you rang the bell. Why don't you let me finish up in the bathroom while you unpack? Then we can talk, maybe even go out to dinner at Frenchy's at our special back table where we can have some privacy."

"Sounds like a plan, Em," Jamie said. Then he stepped over to her, held her shoulders, and kissed her gently on the cheek. He said, "Take your time. I have a feeling that this will be a long night."

Emma closed the bathroom door behind her and gazed at herself in the mirror. Thoughts of what she should say, thoughts of her darling Mo and what he might say or do if he knew Jamie was there all began to race through her mind and became a confusing, overwhelming jumble that truly frightened her.

Emma was a person of little pretense who never worried much about makeup or dolling herself up. Her natural beauty seemed to make anything she wore just perfect. She typically spent ten minutes drying her hair and threw on whatever clothes were handy. That night, she primped everything down to the last detail. By the time she left the bathroom, Jamie had unpacked, showered in the guest bathroom, read the local paper, and had begun to pace the floor. It was 5:30 p.m., and he was starving. When Emma finally appeared, he said, "I called Frenchy's and reserved our table. Francois welcomed me back and wanted to have a little party. I told him that tonight what we needed was quiet and privacy. He understood and said that all would be under control."

Frenchy's was located on a hillside just ten minutes out of town. It commanded a beautiful view of the landscape with the river in the distance.

After they were seated, Jamie said, "It seems almost providential that you picked Frenchy's as the place to go this evening."

"Why is that?" asked Emma.

"Because it could be the one place in Salmon that is symbolic of our future together."

Those last two words gave Emma a chill as an image of Mohammed again appeared in her mind's eye.

"How do you mean, Jamie?"

"I mean that I have just received the CIA assignment of a lifetime. And it's not just for me. It's for you too."

"What? I'm not about to join the CIA."

"Em, I've just received a promotion at least a year before I would have expected one. It came because I was able to do something—I can't tell you what—that no one else had been able to accomplish. Because of this, I have been given a new assignment to a place that you and I have always dreamed about visiting, only now we'll be living there. We will be together in one of the greatest cities in the world and doing it on the government's dime. And not only will we be there together, *full time*, but they have found a job for you teaching first grade at the American school, which just happens to be next door to the American embassy where I will be based. Now we'll even be able to walk to work together, hopefully for years."

At that moment, Francois came to their table and said, "Excuse me, but I just wanted to give you a special welcome-home present." Then from behind his back, he produced a bottle of Dom Pérignon. "For my favorite couple. So good to have you back with us." Then without another word, he produced two champagne flutes and poured this sumptuous vintage for his guests and longtime friends. "Please enjoy," he said and stepped away quietly.

"I guess this couldn't be more apropos," said Jamie. "I'd like to use this vintage to propose a toast to our new future together in *Paree*." He held up his glass and smiled.

Emma, in an obviously mechanical response, did the same, and each then sipped from their glasses.

"You've just dumped a lot on me, Jamie. In a moment's time, you said you want me to pack up, move thousands of miles from home, take a new job, and leave behind everything I've known all my life."

"Well, Em, school here ends in a few weeks, and I have to be there by July first. We will have to sell the house and arrange with the government to get our things moved. We could get everything ready to go while I'm here, and you could stay a while longer to clean things up with the house, help the school find your replacement, and give yourself time to say your goodbyes, and still have some prep time in Paris before the new semester starts there."

Emma didn't know which way to turn. Here was her husband, who a few hours before had turned up without notice barking out plans for her future. No requests for acceptance of these ideas, just an expectation that she'd follow his dictates and change her life without questions and without any consideration on his part for her desires. Now more than ever, she missed Mo—so sweet, so considerate, so kind. Yes, she and Jamie had often dreamed of visiting Paris on a romantic vacation, but living there had never been a consideration.

"Jamie," she finally said, "this all sounds like quite an extraordinary opportunity for you, but did you ever think of asking me if I would want to come along for the ride?"

"No, I just thought it would be perfect for both of us. It's a chance to be part of something totally new and exciting. One thing I've always loved about you was your willingness to try new things. I know you like small-town life, but wouldn't you like to step out of your norms for a while? This assignment won't last forever, and I think you'll come to love the opportunity. And most important, it will give us a chance to do the one thing we've never done since we've been married...be together. It's a chance for us to rekindle what was once the brightest light in our world. We've always had that special love, Em. The last few years have caused it to dim. Now's our chance to get it back. Please be with me on this. It's a special chance, possibly our last chance."

By the time Jamie was finished, Emma was pouring her third glass of champagne. Before she had a chance to respond, Francois reappeared to take their orders. It was a chance to gather her thoughts. When Francois finally left the table, she quietly said, "Jamie, you know how I like to think things over before I respond in any meaningful way. I need to give this idea a great deal of thought. Can we just drop it for now and enjoy our dinner? I'll need a few days, and you'll have to give me that time to sort it all out."

"Sure, Em. I know it's a lot to take in. Take all the time you need."

"Thanks," she said and changed the subject to an update of what had been going on in Salmon since he left. Safe, mundane talk except for one little detail—Mohammed!

Chapter Twenty-Six

It was a strange feeling for Emma. The dinner was wonderful, but the discussion during dinner could be classified as relatively meaningless pap. It was hard for Jamie to put Paris out of his mind to talk about what, to him, was meaningless drivel. For Emma as well, everything felt strained. It was readily apparent to Jamie that not advising Emma of his arrival in advance was, at least in the short term, a serious error.

They were home by 8:00 p.m., with each of them wondering what to do next. Obviously, this kind of homecoming would for most folks be a joyous time with lovemaking an important part of the plan. But there had been no plan, and the raw edges that existed when Jamie left the country still seemed to survive.

Finally, Emma said, "I think I'm going to turn in early, Jamie. I have to be at school by 6:00 a.m. for an all-day field trip that I've set up for my kids. That means I'll be up at 5:00 a.m., and I really have to be fresh for this one."

With that comment, Jamie could sense he might have a warm body next to him that night, but it wouldn't be in motion. "Okay, Em," he managed. "I guess you'll be gone by the time I get up. I'll see you for dinner tomorrow."

"Well," she said, "I don't think so. This trip includes a campfire dinner at the inn. And then I'll be cleaning things up along with a few of the moms. I guess it will be closer to 8:00 or 9:00 before I'm home. Why don't you visit with your folks while I'm gone? I'm sure they'll want to spend time with you."

"Oh, I'm sure you're right about that. I guess I'll just see you when I see you."

"Good night, Jamie," she said. In an instant, she was in the bedroom and under the covers but hardly asleep. All she could think about was Mo and if she could somehow get in touch with him the next day to discuss all that was going on.

*****

As Jamie had suspected, Emma was out of the house when he arose at 7:00 a.m. There wasn't much in the fridge, so he stopped at the bakery, bought some cinnamon rolls, and headed to his parents' home for a breakfast of fresh pastries and coffee. To keep his secret homecoming from Emma, he knew he couldn't tell anyone else, or word surely would have slipped out. This time, however, when his mom opened the door, there was the kind of response he had hoped for from Emma. The look of shock quickly changed to one of elation as she wrapped her arms around her son and couldn't stop hugging him. Soon Jamie's dad appeared, and his hearty handshaking and backslapping kept up the incredibly warm response.

"Hi, guys, it's so good to see you. I just managed to stop by our favorite bakery for some still-warm cinnamon rolls. Let's eat, and I'll tell you everything I can about what's happened and what's coming up."

Finally, Jamie felt like he was experiencing a real homecoming.

By the time he was through retelling what he had told Emma, his parents were just thrilled for both of them. They said they were sure the Steeles—by then their closest friends in Salmon—would be so excited for them even though both sets of parents would miss the couple terribly while they were in Europe.

"Well," said Jamie, "I'm sure you would all like to have reason to travel to Paris, and we'll have R&R occasionally so we can come here to visit you. After all, with the CIA, it's hard to know where or when you'll be posted to a new location. I can tell you honestly that I love the excitement of it all. I just hope Emma will as well."

*****

While Jamie spent the day at his boyhood home, Emma was trying to find a pay phone in her effort to reach Mohammed. The bus stopped two hours into the trip for a bathroom break.

Emma left the parents in charge and ran into a gas station to make the call. She tried three locations before she finally caught up to Mohammed in North Fork.

"Mo," she said, "I don't have much time to talk. We just stopped the bus so the kids could pee. I have to tell you that I'm in shock. Jamie is back. He showed up at the front door yesterday afternoon as I was stepping out of the shower. I have so much to tell you. Do you think you could meet me at your shop tonight around 8:00? I told him I could be out as late as 9:00. I really need your help with this."

"Of course, love. I was expecting to be back around 7:30 and will be there putting together some numbers from today's trip. I'll wait for you."

"Thanks, Mo. I love you. See you tonight."

Chapter Twenty-Seven

The sun had not yet set, so Emma had to be careful as she worked her way over to Mohammed's shop from the school. She made sure she was the last one to leave school, avoiding a walk home with the moms from the trip. Mohammed had left the door open so she could slip in unnoticed. He locked it as soon as she entered. With all the lights out, they embraced, and Emma began to cry.

"Whoa, darling," Mo said, "Nothing has happened yet. Just give me the details so I can work out a plan."

After a minute or two, Emma gathered herself and outlined the details from the moment Jamie arrived until her jumping into bed—alone—the previous night.

"I'm sure he was taken aback when I showed no warmth and never considered making love to him. I hadn't talked to him since last night because he was sleeping when I left this morning. He probably took my suggestion about spending the day with his parents. But now I have to go home and face him again, and I don't know what to say or how to avoid making love with him tonight."

"Tell you what, Em, maybe I can help for tonight by breaking up the party. Why don't you just say that you ran into me as you were coming back from school, and I was returning from my trip? When you told me about my 'best buddy's' return, I just couldn't wait to come over and catch up. I'll stay as late as possible while you later excuse yourself because you're so tired after getting up so early for the field trip and having such a long day. That way, I'll have a chance to work out a strategy that we can discuss tomorrow."

"Mo, you're just a lifesaver," Emma said. "Let's go now. It's almost 9:00 and I'd like to be under the covers by 10:00. I just wish it was with you."

They hugged and left for Emma's house.

Five minutes later, Emma unlocked the door. As they stepped in, the aroma of pizza and beer filled the air. In a moment, Jamie appeared with a cold one in his hand, though it surely wasn't his first. Bleary-eyed, he spotted Mohammed, broke into a broad grin, and then staggered slightly as he rushed to greet his old friend.

"Hey, Mo, you old fart!" he shouted. "I was thinking about you all day. Emma tells me you're the biggest cleaning tycoon in Idaho. Says you're richer than Crises. Maybe I should be offering you some fine wine, but best I can do for you is pizza and beer. Help yourself, my man."

Jamie said all this with obviously slurred words. As the three of them walked back into the kitchen to attack the pizza, they noticed six empty bottles lined up on the sink. As Jamie rattled on, Emma managed to say a premature good night. It wasn't until midnight that Mohammed managed to leave after rehearing from Jamie all the details about Paris and Jamie's future with Emma. It was a hard story for him to hear, and he began to contemplate how he would sabotage Jamie's plan.

Chapter Twenty-Eight

Once again, Emma managed to leave for school before Jamie awoke. He didn't rise until 10:00 a.m., with a throbbing headache thanks to the previous night's activities. With no special plan for the day, he decided to walk around town to see if he could find some old school buddies until Emma came home.

At the same time, Mohammed was at work but hardly working. He was trying to outline a plan whereby Emma could ultimately decline Jamie's offer and ask for a divorce.

While this plan was coming together, Jamie's parents managed to reach the Steeles, who were away on a brief vacation, to tell them Jamie was back and with an exciting new job and plans for their kids' future together. Jamie's mom was determined to have a homecoming party and wanted to be sure their best friends would be back in time. As it turned out, they planned to be back in just two days and couldn't wait to see Jamie and hear all the news.

While these wheels were turning, Emma, the one with the most anguish, was trying to stay focused at school. From the looks on her student's faces, she knew she must not be making sense at times. Finally, one of her favorite six-year-olds said, "Mrs. Duncan, are you okay? You're really talking sorta funny."

The whole class giggled, and Emma struggled to find a sensible response.

"Oh, I'm fine, Janie," she stammered. "I'm just a little tired after our field trip yesterday."

"Oh," said Janie, "I guess you must be getting old."

The whole class, including Emma, cracked up.

When the bell rang at 3:00 p.m., Emma was the first one out of the room. Fortunately, she did have cleaning to pick up, so she could meet Mohammed at his shop on the up-and-up. His assistant was home sick, so Mo had to handle everything. As Emma entered, the only other customer was just leaving. When they were alone, Emma asked if Mo had come up with a plan. As he was about to explain the concept, his father entered unexpectedly and in a foul mood.

"Mohammed, I must speak with you at once on an urgent matter," his father said. He then said a terse hello to Emma and asked that they might have some privacy. Mohammed shrugged his shoulders and said, "Business matters, Emma. See you soon."

"Sure," she responded and said her good-byes as she exited the premises. *Now what?* she thought to herself. *I'm going home unarmed and don't know when Mo can get back to me. I don't see his father very often, but he's always been very pleasant. He sure looked serious today.*

In fact, his father was deadly serious. He had received word from Iran that something new and troublesome was going on. The mullahs said they suspected the United States, through the CIA, was trying to undermine the government, but they were not exactly sure what was happening. However, they did know one thing, money was getting tighter, and they were asking IGO to become more aggressive in their fund-raising. So now Mohammed's dad wanted him to become more directly involved in soliciting contributions from other countrymen now residing in the United States. His father and his dear friend, Ali Hassan, were going to take a trip back to Canada to put the arm on some of their former countrymen.

Mohammed was given a list with more than five hundred names to contact and plead their case. Now he could see that his typical twelve-hour days would increase to sixteen hours plus weekends to do the job he had pledged to do.

Chapter Twenty-Nine

Two days had passed. Jamie hadn't pushed Emma for an answer about Paris but was about to. Mohammed had essentially disappeared from the scene, buried in his extra work. He did manage to reach Emma by phone to tell her he had a plan, but there was a serious and unexpected business problem that both he and his dad had to resolve that would take all his time for the next week or two. He pleaded with her to hold on until they could find a time to be together privately.

*****

With this news, Emma was terribly worried and torn over what she would do. And the next night, the couple's parents were throwing Jamie's homecoming party. She watched them as they prepared everything and how excited they were for their kids and their future together.

They were talking about saving up to make a trip together to Paris and to see as much of Europe as they could afford. They had even gone to the post office to apply for passports.

With all this going on, Emma began to feel distraught—even a little evil. If ever they were to find out what she and Mo had been up to, their worlds would collapse, and with that, so would hers.

*****

Jamie had now been home for five days and yet to lay a hand on his wife. As they left their home on the way to the party, Jamie finally asked her about Paris.

"Em," he said, "you asked for a few days to think about the future. This is day five, and you have yet to say a word. In fact, we've hardly spent more time together since I've been back than when I was thousands of miles away. Do you have any questions, or have you made a decision? I think I have a right to know."

They kept walking, and as they approached the Duncans' front door, Emma said, "Tomorrow is Saturday. We'll have all day to talk it out. Can we wait until then?"

"Okay, 'til tomorrow," Jamie responded as they came into what was an extraordinarily happy place.

From then until 1:00 a.m., it was hugs and kisses, great food and drink, and the warmth of family that finally made things seem right again, normal, the way home and family was supposed to be.

As they slipped under the sheets that night, Jamie moved toward Emma, put his arm across her chest, and rolled her over so that they lay together face-to-face for the first time since his return.

"It was good tonight, Em," he said softly. "It was the first time in ages that my best girl was back to being her beautiful self. I can't tell you how much I've missed the real you. I love you so much. Please give us a chance."

With that, he came close and planted a soft kiss on her lips. She didn't back away but didn't exactly respond either. Inside, she was tied up in knots. But then, Jamie pressed on, and Emma found herself succumbing to his expert kisses. He gently caressed her as he had so many times before. When the night finally ended, Emma had made love to her husband for the first time in what seemed to be forever and was more confused than ever before. And the next day was D-Day.

Chapter Thirty

Jamie was asleep in a moment, his arm across Emma as she stared at the ceiling, her mind cycling over and over all that had gone on from the time she waved good-bye to Jamie as he was on his way to Saudi Arabia until the last tender moment she had just experienced. *What would have happened*, she thought, *if Mo had been available*? Would she be in bed with him now if he had laid it on the line to Jamie? And if he had, what would their parents have said? She knew they would all be horrified if their affair became known. What would Jamie have done to Mo? He was much bigger and stronger than Mo, and he had gone through all sorts of training in the army and CIA. He probably could kill someone with his bare hands. *Fear* was the operational word—fear of hurt to the parents, to Mo, to their friends. Emma unconsciously began to curl her body into a tight ball. Every nerve ending was taut and ready to spring. Then suddenly, Jamie started to talk in his sleep. She looked into his face. In the dark, she could see him smiling and heard him say over and over, "I love you, Em. I love you, Em" until finally he rolled over and was silent again.

She looked at the clock. It was 3:00 a.m., and she yearned for sleep, but there was no way it would come. She had to talk with Mo and be reassured, so she slipped out of bed and tiptoed out of the room, closing the door behind her, and went to the kitchen telephone. She dialed Mo's number and let it ring for at least a minute, but no one answered. *Where could he be?* she thought. This whole secretive situation with his business was becoming stranger by the day, and his lack of contact with her was completely out of character.

She hung up the phone, went back to bed, and stared at the ceiling until finally sleep came at 4:00 a.m. The alarm went off at 7:00 a.m. Emma was exhausted. Jamie, on the other hand, awoke with a smile on his face. He turned and looked at Emma who promptly pulled the pillow over her face and moaned with an expression of agony that had the special kind of intensity that could come only from a person who was tormented both mentally and physically by her desperate circumstances. Never in her life had she ever dreamed of being a married woman in a love triangle, with her husband and childhood sweetheart on one hand and her other best friend from childhood on the other. From the all-American boy to the Iranian immigrant, it all sounded too strange to believe, and she yearned for it to disappear and allow her to awake from the nightmare she had allowed to happen.

Chapter Thirty-One

Ali, Samir, and Ibrahim were quickly into the development of specific plans to make major changes in Iran. Ali had already developed detailed and extensive plans for a coup that would remove the mullahs from political power while still allowing them to remain as leaders of the Shiite majority. It was a delicate sort of compromise that allowed for the majority religion of the country to be respected but for its political influence to be excised in favor of a secular group of twelve leaders.

Samir and Ibrahim were among the group of twelve, all lifelong friends, who would become the leadership group. From them, a prime minister, president, and vice president would be selected, with the rest likely to form a cabinet and write a new constitution for the country. They were a talented, largely professional group, highly educated in Europe and, to a lesser degree, the United States. The key man in this plan was to be Mustafa, the one friend of this group who had taken his religious bent and used it to promote himself into the group of ruling mullahs. The twelve men all counted Mustafa as one of their own even though he lived according to the strict Sharia lifestyle. The trick to the entire plan would be to woo him to their side.

As the mullah leadership went, Mustafa was likely the most moderate. He would even attend social events with his old friends and maintained relationships with them. The plan was for Samir, in a one-on-one conversation, to convince Mustafa that while he and all their friends believed in Allah and observed and cared about the Shiite practice of Islam, they felt religious observance should be kept in the mosque and in the home, not in the government. This concept, he would say, would be in line with the great majority of Iranians. It would allow people to express themselves in terms of religion as well as in a more socially honest way while, at the same time, reopening access to the world at large for Iran, then a taboo in the world community.

While Samir was thrilled at the thought of where these ideas would carry both his group and his country, he shivered at the idea of submitting them to his old friend. Would he even consider the proposal, or would he dismiss it out of hand? Would he listen calmly or call the police and have Samir and his family arrested along with all the others? So much was riding on this encounter. The night before his meeting with Mustafa, he rehearsed everything over and over again. Soya watched him and became increasingly nervous. She had never seen him so intense. Finally, she approached him, put her arms around him, and held him close. He responded in kind and then began to cry. His body shook with fear—not so much for himself, but for his wife and children and all their friends should things go wrong.

That night, they lay together, looking into each other's eyes, valuing their love, and just wanting to feel each other's warmth, knowing full well that it could be their last night together.

Chapter Thirty-Two

Mohammed had yet to become available. Emma was becoming panicked. She owed Jamie an answer and promised it would come that day. Thoughts about the wonderful night the families had just had together kept cycling through her mind. Then there was Jamie's expert, tender lovemaking. Finally, there were the thoughts of what a breakup would do to her family and Jamie's. They had all become so close. The hurt would be so penetrating. And now Mohammed, always her anchor and currently her lover, had mysteriously disappeared from the scene just when she needed him most.

Poor Emma. She had always thought herself to be strong and in control of her life, but now she was like a child lost at sea. As she sat gazing out at the backyard, wondering what was to become of her, she felt a light tap on her shoulder.

"Morning, Em," said Jamie. "Quite a night, wasn't it? Really special."

"I guess," she replied in a somewhat somber tone.

"Something wrong, babe?" he asked.

"No, not really."

"Good," he said. "What say I go to the bakery for some of their world-famous croissants while you make us some coffee and OJ? Then we can talk about what's to come. Okay?"

"Okay. See you back here in ten."

Jamie left. Emma pondered, but in her heart, she knew what she had to do. She loved Mo dearly, but for all she knew, he could be in Timbuktu. No calls in days. No contact of any kind. And now her husband and previous love of her life was back and offering to make things right in a very real way in a way that would take away all the potential hurt that would come if she were to run off and eventually marry Mo.

When Jamie returned, Emma let out a deep breath, went over to him, put her arms around his neck, and simply said, "Okay. I'm in."

With those three words, Jamie picked her up and swung her in circles around the room. It felt to him much like it did when Stu gave him the news that he was leaving Iran for Paris—a tremendous weight had been lifted from his shoulders.

They sat, they ate, they smiled, and they talked nonstop about their future. It was sort of like the first day they met in high school. Nonstop chatter was the order of the day, followed by hours of lovemaking that seemed to renew all the bonds that had been so terribly broken.

Chapter Thirty-Three

Mo felt as though he was suddenly catapulted into another world. If he wasn't working at the office, he was on one call after another, literally begging people he didn't know to give hundreds if not thousands of dollars to Iran. It was truly like pulling teeth. Most said what he had said, "We're US citizens now. We can't be supporting a country that held our people hostage and that has no relationship with our new country. They've become the enemy!"

After pleading his case over and over again, even these folks agreed to part with a few dollars, most of them on a "cash only" basis so their contributions couldn't be traced.

Fortunately, there was enough of a still-loyal base that after contacting more than two-thirds of his list, he had managed to acquire $2 million in donations. About one hundred fifty contacts still remained, some of them among the wealthiest of the group. His father said their homeland expected at least $5 million in donations from the American and Canadian loyalists. They were making headway but still had at least another week of calls to make.

The thought of another week of this was torture to Mo. He was so worried about Em and what was going on with her and Jamie, but his time was totally spoken for. He only hoped she would find a way to hold Jamie off until he could devote his full time to her—his dear love and light of his life. Surely, there couldn't have been a worse time for Mo's father to have called on him, but he couldn't say no to him; he just had to pray it would all work out.

It had been ten days since Emma and Mo had spoken when he came home at midnight to find his answering machine blinking. Mo pressed the play button, and this is what he heard:

> *My dearest Mo, making this call may be the most difficult thing I have ever done, and I'm not quite sure how to say what I must say to you. It has been ten long days since I've heard from you. As you must know, I've left several messages for you that have gone unanswered. In all the time that we've known each other, I've never known you not to call back in short order. Now while I've found myself in dire need of your support, I've heard nothing from you. I don't understand your nonresponse when you know how critical these days have been.*
>
> *The upshot of all this is that after the welcome-home party at Jamie's parents' house, things between Jamie and me started to improve. I also faced the stark reality of how difficult a divorce would be on our families, who have now become best friends. In any event, Jamie began to press me in bed that night to make love to him and to give*

him an answer about Paris. Long story short, I caved. Without you there and with no idea where you were and what was going on with what you described as "business problems," I had to make a decision.

Mo, I don't know if this was the right decision, but it seemed so at the time. You know I love you dearly, but you've simply disappeared. In any event, I'm going to go to Paris and hope that everything works out for the best for all three of us. I'll do my best to stay in touch, but please don't contact me now. I just couldn't bear it. I've been so torn, and if I saw you again, it would only cause more anguish and pain. Please let me try to reconcile without interference. When we're settled a while in Paris, I'll be in touch with you. Good-bye for now.

Mo felt as though he had been stabbed through the heart. At first, there was a sharp pain and then numbness. He didn't know how long he sat there staring at the wall, but when he looked at his wristwatch, more than half an hour had passed.

Emma had asked him not to call, but how could he not? Yet the last thing he would ever do was hurt the girl he loved so dearly. He felt like choking his father. He knew it wasn't a fair thought—his dad had no idea what was going on between him and Em—yet that terrible thought still came to him. Were it not for this IGO project, he could be on track to have his Emma forever. Now, unfortunately, she was likely forever lost.

At this moment of severe depression, his phone rang. It was his father checking on his progress. It was all he could do to keep from shouting and hanging up on him, but he managed, barely, to keep his equilibrium. When he finally hung up, he decided to bury himself in calling the rest of the people on the list and hoping that something—anything—would happen to change the situation. He knew it would take a miracle.

Chapter Thirty-Four

The day arrived that Samir was to meet with Mustafa. The pretext for the meeting was to arrange a fiftieth birthday party for their friend Ibrahim. While this was a real plan, Samir's intent was to quickly segue the conversation from a birthday party to a political party. He wanted to first get a sense of how far Mustafa would be willing to go if, in fact, he would listen to the group's ideas at all.

Ken and Samir went through multiple rehearsals of the conversation with Ken acting the part of Mustafa. He posed surprise questions to Samir to see how he would tackle unexpected responses to their ideas. By noon on that critical day, Ken was satisfied that Samir would be able to handle the challenge. It was game on.

At 2:00 p.m., Mustafa arrived at Samir's home. He was warmly greeted by Soya and the three boys, who had always thought of him as a loving uncle. He would play with them, tell them stories, and give them warm hugs whenever they were together. It was a genuine sense of family for him.

After an hour of play with the boys, Soya led them away so that the men could talk privately. Samir and Mustafa spent half an hour reviewing plans for Ibrahim's birthday party, including the guest list, menu, and entertainment. When the basics were settled, Samir changed the tone of

the conversation when he inquired about a recent judg-
ment by the high court regarding a "political enemy" who
was sentenced to death for supposedly committing adultery. He was to be beheaded while the adulteress was to be
stoned to death in public.

"Tell me, Mustafa, in the twentieth century, what are
your personal feelings regarding these forms of punishment, especially for this class of crime?"

Mustafa looked up at Samir and then down again. For
a minute or two, he was consumed in thought. Then he
stood and began to pace the room. After several minutes,
he finally responded to Samir's question. "You ask, Samir,
a question about a subject that I have often debated in my
own mind. There are certain things in the Koran about
which I have observed more than one interpretation. Those
who take the book that guides our lives in the strictest terms
also tend to be the harshest in interpreting the correct way
that things should be handled. Others of us, however, have
a more liberal bent and wish to take the words as guidelines
for living as good men but in ways that make sense for the
times we now live in. Surely, adultery is not something I
can abide. However, in my mind, a reasonable time in jail
to consider what one has done, as well as a year of religious
retraining, would seem a more reasonable approach. The
embarrassment alone would likely be the worst part for the
participants. Archaic and extreme punishments like public
beheading and stoning are not right to my way of thinking. However, I must tell you that my more moderate way
is very much in the minority among the ruling group of

mullahs. Even I must be careful of what I say, lest I be the object of severe punishment myself."

This last comment gave Samir pause. He thought, *Just how influential, I wonder, is my dear friend? If he is among a small minority when it comes to such punishments, does he have the power to make the top men even consider a change in the politics of the country? I better stop this direction of the conversation and share my concern with Ali before I push forward.*

"Come, Mustafa. The day is passing quickly, and Soya has planned an early dinner for us so that you can return to the mosque for evening prayer."

"Ah, your wife is so kind, Samir. Every time I have the pleasure of visiting your home, she makes it a true joy. And those boys...there are none better. I can't thank you enough for being such a dear and lifelong friend."

Chapter Thirty-Five

Mo made the last call on the list—saved the best for last, as the expression goes. This was a contribution from a man named Hamid, the wealthiest of all the Iranian immigrants in the United States. He had inherited great oil wealth from his family and then decided to get away from the shah and his group of thieves by moving to the United States just a couple of years before the return of the mullahs. He was a bit younger, and while he still loved his homeland, he loved living in freedom even more.

Mo's father had collected $1.8 million in Canada. Before calling Hamid, Mo had reached $3 million in contributions. He told Hamid of their goal and how close they were in achieving it if only he would help. Hamid wired $200,000 from an account he maintained in Canada as soon as they were off the phone. Finally, the nightmare of this three-week-long solicitation was over.

Mo's father came to his house the next day. He was all smiles and so proud of their effort. "I knew you would come through for me, my son," he said. "I know how hard it is to ask for more, but our country is in need, and we had to do our part. I understand that along with other groups from around the world, we've collected $25 million to help the cause. It may not seem like that much, but we need every dollar to maintain our position in the world."

Mo's father wanted to go for a celebratory dinner, but Mo declined, claiming exhaustion and the need for sleep. Thankfully, his father didn't push it. He just hugged Mo, thanked him again, and left him to his bed and his endless thoughts of Emma.

The next morning, Mo saw her drive past his shop on the way to the airport with Jamie. He had heard Jamie was leaving for Paris first with Emma to follow the next week. Their house was sold in just three days, and the government was to pick up all their belongings the next day. Emma would then stay with her folks for a few days to tie up loose ends before heading off for a new life.

On several evenings, after dark, Mo would hide in a small forested area near the Steele's home to see if Emma would come by. He did manage to see her at a distance twice before she left. It was everything he could do to keep from calling out to her, but he managed to hold his emotions inside.

On the last day Emma was to be in town; Mo arrived at his shop at 7:00 a.m. He had just raised the shades in the front window, and at that instant, he saw Mr. Steele's station wagon zoom by with Emma and her mom inside and lots of luggage piled in the back. For Mo, it was a moment of profound sadness.

Chapter Thirty-Six

Ken was anxious to hear the result of Samir's meeting. When he saw the glum look on his new friend's face, he felt a tinge of disappointment.

"Tell me, Samir," he started, "what came of the meeting with Mustafa?"

Slowly, Samir related his concerns, along with the abiding fears he continued to have for his family.

"I understand your concerns, Samir, but the truth is that he is our only chance. If he cannot move things along, we likely won't have an opportunity to change things. This is where the risk factor we all knew was there might come into play. But if he admits, as he did, that he would rather not continue with the kind of extremism that has existed, then we at least have a chance. I must beg you to go back to him and be honest about your intent. If he cares as much for you and your family as he claims, I seriously doubt he will put any of you in harm's way."

As was his fashion, Samir took in Ken's words and contemplated the possibilities in silence. Was he taking on all this risk more on behalf of the Americans or of his own people? Could he imagine the rest of his life spent in jail or worse? Was it worth destroying a lifelong friendship and risking everything to move ahead with his moral agenda?

Finally, he spoke, "I must weigh everything very carefully, Ali, given these new circumstances. Please give me a week. I will contact you as soon as I have reviewed everything with all my friends and advise you as to our decision. We must consider all possibilities, and if we move ahead, do everything to mitigate risk."

"I understand, Samir. But time is also a consideration. Please let me know no later than a week from today."

"I promise you, Ali, that I will. And thank you for your patience."

When Ken returned to his current safe house, he found a coded message that piqued his curiosity. It seemed that US Intelligence had picked up information on an influx of cash to the Iranian government from a variety of overseas sources. Apparently, they had been tapping the phone of someone suspicious in the United States. In surveilling this person, they had picked up a phone conversation with another American in a rural Idaho location. The conversation dealt with making a sizeable contribution to a group called IGO. The people in Washington had checked it out and found it registered as a charity that benefitted US military veterans. The history of IGO's contributions weren't significant in terms of dollar amounts, but there was no sign of impropriety until now. Over the past few years, total receipts from IGO were $50,000. The contribution promised to them by this individual alone was $200,000. The sum and substance of it was that they wanted Ken, as part of his assignment in-country, to see if he could learn more about this group and, perhaps, any others that might be helping to boost the economy of Iran.

Chapter Thirty-Seven

Jamie was waiting in the arrival section at Orly Airport. When he saw Emma coming out of customs, he waved frantically, jumping up and down to get her attention. When she finally saw him, she smiled but couldn't move very quickly with the two extremely large suitcases she had in tow. As soon as she came to him, he picked her up off her feet and hugged her tightly.

"We're actually here babe, in Paris together, at last, for the long haul. You can't believe how beautiful it is, and you also won't believe the apartment they gave us. It's literally one block away from your school and a block and a half from the embassy entrance. It faces a beautiful street lined with plane trees, and most importantly, there are incredible bakeries and food shops everywhere. I just can't wait to show you everything I've found, and I've just scratched the surface. And—"

"Whoa, boy, I just came in," Emma interrupted. "I'm jet-lagged, and all I want to do is lie down for a bit. Then you can tell me all these things again when I can take it in. It all sounds great, honey, but let me just take a breath."

"Sorry, Em. I'm just so excited about everything but didn't have you here to share it with me. Let's just get you home, unpacked, and rested. I just hope you don't mind if I give you lots of hugs and kisses just for being here."

"Hugs and kisses are always welcome. They've been far too long in coming, and I certainly won't stop them. Not ever!"

Emma had begun to nod off on the cab ride home. As they approached the American embassy and Emma's new school, Jamie gave her a nudge.

"Here's where we'll be working, Em," he whispered.

She opened her eyes and looked in awe at the beautiful embassy, the American school, and the tree-lined street that seemed to create both a regal and romantic aura at the same time. She sat up straight.

"Our apartment is just ahead," said Jamie. "Right there, on the corner." He pointed at a typical Parisian apartment building standing four stories high. The cab pulled up in front to drop them off.

As they entered the lobby, Jamie said, "The elevator is small. It should have enough room for you and your suitcases. We're on the top floor with north and east views and a corner window where we can look out on the Eiffel Tower. I'll run up the stairs and be waiting for you when you get to the top."

In a flash, Jamie did the stairs two at a time and was waiting when the somewhat ancient elevator arrived. He picked up the suitcases and led Emma down the hall to their new home.

Even in her somewhat hazy state, it was all very exciting. But what she really wanted was a few hours of shut-eye and a return to her own vivacious self.

Emma awoke at seven in the evening. Jamie gave her a quick tour of the apartment, showed her how to operate the rather outdated bathroom fixtures, and gave her some privacy while she showered and prepared for the first truly French dinner of her life.

"Thanks, honey, for letting me sleep. Now I'm really ready to eat. The airline food was just awful!" Emma said. "I'm ready to leave."

"I know," Jamie said. "We'll just walk down the street to my favorite bistro for a casual dinner. It really doesn't matter much where you go. The food is just fabulous most anyplace."

"Great," said Emma. "I'm ready to eat my way through France. I have a feeling I should let out all the waistlines in my closet just to get ready."

"Oh no, Em, you can't lose your girlish figure just when I finally have the chance, after all these years, to take advantage of that beautiful body."

"So now you want to trade one kind of fun for another, eh? Well, okay, I'll compromise. I promise not to ask for seconds on dessert."

"Hmm," said Jamie, "let's cross the street here. I don't want you walking by my favorite bakery."

At that, Emma started to run full speed down the street, and Jamie didn't catch her until she suddenly stopped and turned to face a window filled with fabulous pastries and beautiful breads. She stood, slack-jawed, as she took it all in.

"Uh-oh," she said. "Now I'm in serious trouble!"

"I told you, babe. Now you're going to say you won't ask for thirds."

Jamie grabbed Emma's hand, then put his arm around her shoulder as they walked happily onto dinner.

Chapter Thirty-Eight

Three days had passed without a word from Samir. With his primary project temporarily in limbo, Ken had started to investigate IGO. Beyond what he had gotten from the coded message, he seemed to have hit a solid wall. The two lower-level local contacts knew nothing of the organization (or at least that's what they claimed), and he had yet to broach the subject with Samir and his friends.

With little to go on and not much else of interest happening, he decided to take a wild stab and contact Jamie in Paris. Maybe he had some inside knowledge that could help him in cracking the case. Coded messaging to Jamie slowed things down a bit as he had been out of town on assignment.

*****

It took two days for his message to catch up with his predecessor at his Paris office. It read,

> Jamie, I received a message from Washington about an outfit known as IGO. We don't know if the name itself has any significance, but we do know that

it is registered with the government as a charitable group and that it contributes money to the benefit of the US military, especially veterans groups. We know that in the few years they've been around, they've given a total of roughly $50,000 to their cause. However, there was a suspicious Iranian who is now a naturalized American citizen whose phone we were tapping. He is a wealthy man who we heard being solicited for a sizeable contribution to IGO. In the course of this conversation, he agreed to contribute $200,000. Now that's just one man and one contribution that is four times the size of all IGO's contributions over the past few years. Oh, and another thing, the guy making the phone call was traced back to a small town in rural Idaho called Salmon. Now, don't you hail from that neck of the woods? I wouldn't think there would be many Iranians in that area. Please advise if you can help me with this.

As he read the message, Jamie was stunned. An image of Mohammed came into his mind, and all he wanted to do was shut it out. The last thing he could imagine was Mo hurting his adopted country, but with no more than a dozen Iranians in Salmon and not many more likely to be in the entire state, he knew that Mo, while perhaps not a participant, was likely to be aware of such an effort. For now, though, he didn't want to say anything, so this was how he responded to Ken:

> That is my neck of the woods, but as you say, there sure aren't many Iranians in Idaho. Let me see if I can learn anything, and if I do, I'll get back to you.

"Thanks, Jamie," came a message in reply. "We're sort of stumped for now, so anything you might be able to do would be appreciated."

Jamie needed to catch his breath. He also thought this might be a situation where Emma might be of help. The only thing was he had to be careful about giving away anything that might be considered classified.

When he came home that night, Emma, in a sparkling mood, welcomed him with a huge hug and a magnificent dinner provided by her new hobby-lessons in French cooking. This was her first try, and the aroma made Jamie momentarily forget the travails of the day. He proceeded directly to the small closet where they did their best to properly store a few bottles of their favorite wines. For the leg of lamb that Emma had prepared, a fine burgundy seemed like just the ticket. Jamie had squirreled away a Charmes-Chambertin when he had first arrived in Paris, and this seemed like the perfect occasion to open it.

Two hours and two helpings of everything later, a much-distended Jamie reclined on the sofa with Emma at his side, each of them holding a glass of their last treasured sips of wine.

Jamie came back to his worries of the day. While he hated to break the mood, he knew he couldn't rest until he bounced his concerns off Emma. When he decided to put it to her, he said, "Em, when I was away in Saudi, did you have a chance to spend much time with Mo?"

Emma didn't move her body, but her eyes suddenly popped open. "Oh," she said, "we did see each other probably once or twice a week. I would see him at his shop when I brought in cleaning, and sometimes we would have coffee or occasionally go to dinner. He really was a good and supportive friend when you were gone. You know, just like he always was."

Her tone and words made it all seem innocent, and the relationship, while close, essentially innocuous.

"Tell me, Em, did he ever talk about Iran or any of the stuff going on there? Anything about politics? The religious group that runs the country or anything like that?"

"Gee, Jamie, not that I remember. That sounds more like something that his dad or some of the other older men who lived there much of their lives would be interested in. Mo was just a little boy when they moved to Canada and not too much older when they came to Salmon. I doubt that he feels much, if any, connection to his homeland. Why do you ask?"

"Well, I can't say exactly, but the CIA is always checking on Iranian politics, and I thought he might be a source for some background information. But I think you're right. I don't think he cares much about Iran. I don't remember him saying anything about it either. I think his only concern was his social status with the girls who always thought of him as an outsider. He used to tell me how badly he wanted to get laid in high school but that none of the girls were even interested in making out with him, except his dad's friend's daughter, and he didn't care much for her."

Emma gulped but didn't say a word. Jamie, on the other hand, still had a gut feeling that Mo or others in his family must somehow be involved. He was between the proverbial rock and a hard place—his best childhood friend and the CIA.

Chapter Thirty-Nine

The day of reckoning had arrived for Samir and his friends. They had been meeting for several days and finally arrived at the conclusion that if they were unable to move the political mountain, it was unlikely any other group would be able to do it. With fear ever present upon their faces, they stood in a circle, arms around one another, and pledged to do everything in their power to make it happen.

Samir called Ken to arrange the next meeting. Once again, Ken arrived at Samir's home, this time after nightfall, to arrange the next move.

"Come in, Ali," said Samir. They shook hands, and Ken could feel a slight tremble in Samir's grip to go along with the intense look on his face. They walked swiftly to his underground office where he and Ibrahim informed Ken of their decision.

"Gentlemen," said Ken, "I'm so glad you have all agreed to move forward, so let's get down to business. We must first go back to Mustafa. He really is the key to everything and our only direct access to the mullahs. I would hope that he would be able to create a situation in our favor through diplomatic channels but, frankly, the more likely course would be in the form of a coup. The United States, of course, would provide whatever military assistance we would need, if any, but the better circumstance would be one where we turn the leader of the Republican Guard against the strict theocrats and toward a more secular regime. That is not to say that the theocrats need to be killed or imprisoned, just moved into the mosques, if you will, and out of the political leadership. We're not interested in bloodshed here, just a return to civility and normalized political intercourse."

Ken set out the details of the plan. Once again, Mustafa would return to Samir's home, this time with all the friends involved in the plot. Wives and children would also be in attendance to make the atmosphere of the evening less businesslike as they celebrated Ibrahim's birthday party. The plan was to get Mustafa relaxed so that, after dinner, the men could go off, as was the custom, to talk among themselves. The others would guide the conversation toward politics and the strategy to change the direction of the country. Because this was a busy group of men, the first date when everyone could come together was three weeks away. The gun was cocked; in three weeks, it would be time to pull the trigger.

Chapter Forty

Three weeks passed. As days went by, anxiety among the group of friends began to grow.

Samir was reminded of a particular image he remembered from his travels to Europe—*The Last Supper*. He wondered if there would be a Judas amongst them.

On the day of the party, the weather was comfortable, and the day bright with sunshine. Following afternoon prayers, the sizeable group began to gather. Soon the sounds of joy and laughter, accompanied by music dating back to their childhoods and beyond, began to pierce the air. For all but the twelve key players—a mixture of successful businessmen, lawyers, doctors, and university professors— the atmosphere was pure joy. For them, it was a matter of maintaining a false front to cover myriad concerns.

The hours passed. The sumptuous feast concluded, and the key men separated themselves from the crowd and recongregated in a small guesthouse at the edge of Samir's property. For a while, talk of their childhood days continued the mood of camaraderie. Finally, at a moment when the conversation began to quiet, Samir stood and spoke to the group in a way to command their attention. He then turned to face Mustafa and address him directly.

"Mustafa, my dear friend and comrade to all here, I, as representative of this special group of lifelong friends, want to address a most important issue. It is an area of thought where all of us seem to be of like mind as it relates to our government and its manner of rule…a manner that we think should be adjusted to better relate both to our own citizens and the world at large.

"All of us, dear friend, believe in following the teachings of the Koran. All of us pray to Allah as prescribed each day for his blessings and goodwill. We believe in peace and friendship and love just as we have demonstrated it this day. What concerns us is that we and others for reasons of which we may not even be aware could be severely punished by a small group of men who run this country with an iron fist, keeping virtually everyone in a state of sublimated if not overt fear. They have also managed to isolate us both politically and economically from key countries around the world because of our political stance. Even though the few men in this room represent the upper class of our current society, we seemingly have no ability whatsoever to change the status quo. Only you, Mustafa, among all of us, have access to the mullahs that have changed our government into a strict theocracy. Now we know that you, even with your stature among this group, do not have the ability or level of status on your own to effect a change to a more democratic method of governance. However, we also know that you have become very close with the leader of the Republican Guard. And while the Ayatollah Khomeini has theoretical control, without the Republican Guard to back him, he only has true power within the confines of the mosque."

Samir paused, then continued, "Mustafa, we are all aware that what I am about to propose to you could land all of us in jail, or worse, probably much worse. We in this room strongly believe that profound change is necessary, and with the cooperation of the Republican Guard, it could happen. I hesitate to call it a coup, as the mullahs would remain the religious leaders of the country. This is as it should be. We also feel that your more moderate bent among this group might endear them far more to our populace. We can envision a day, our dear friends, of a democratically elected group to run the government as politicians should while our religious leaders tend to the business of religious leadership and not that of running a government."

All eyes were on Mustafa. No one knew if he would burst out of the room or bless them.

All the positive emotions of the day were fresh and stored up in the souls of each man. Each moment that passed seemed like an eternity before Mustafa rose and faced Samir and his other lifelong friends.

Mustafa began, "I know that what has just been put forth to me was not something blurted out on the spur of the moment. I have known all of you for a lifetime and can say that all of you are thoughtful and caring men with great substance. I also know that your passion for this cause must be very deep to state your feelings openly to me knowing that it could be very dangerous indeed to reveal such thoughts. So in return, I must be honest with you. Among the ten key men that run our country, the Ayatollah Khomeini controls 90 percent of the power. The rest of us share the somewhat feckless remainder. Without his say-so, no change that you might suggest will occur. Not only will he not allow change, he will also not relinquish power. I will tell you that none of the other ruling body of mullahs would likely listen to anything you are suggesting. The truth is that all of you and your families would be arrested and executed if you were to try any of this. Now you suggest that I should approach my friend, General Abdullah, the head of the Republican Guard. Let me tell you that this is truly an all-or-nothing play. If he were inclined to go along-he is not a terribly religious man-then he would likely do so only if he were to become the president and rule the roost. Once there, with the expected loyalty of the guard, he would be most difficult to replace."

Mustafa paused, considering, then continued, "On the other hand, if he were not inclined and decided that his current position is too cozy to risk, he would no doubt give me up to the ruling body for sanctions to be followed quickly by execution."

As those words sank in, Mustafa added, "Please keep in mind, my friends, that while I'm a strict believer in our religious laws, I also believe in the concept of the separation between church and state. I, like most of you, have had the opportunity to travel to the United States and marvel at the success of their method of government. But is it worth the risk? This is no small question for any of us. Let me leave you with this. I must think deeply about what you are suggesting here. There will be much prayer and soul-searching involved. However, you should not have concern about my loyalty to you as lifelong friends. I respect you, even more, today for your honesty and strength in stepping forward. While it will no doubt take me some time, I promise to get back to you in due course with an answer. Until then, I must ask that not a word of what has been discussed in this room pass beyond these four walls. This includes your wives and children, whom you will have committed to this dangerous venture should we proceed."

With these words, Mustafa stepped toward Samir and embraced him. As he did so, he whispered in his ear, "It is you I will contact with my decision, dear friend." He then waved good-bye to the group and showed himself out.

When the door closed behind him, an audible sigh of relief permeated the room. At first, no one spoke. Then Ibrahim rose and said, "My dearest friends, let me first thank you for the incredible birthday party. At fifty years of age, I am the eldest of our group, and while age does not necessarily cause wisdom, let me say to all of you that what we have done today is what wise men do. We have spoken the truth to power. We have taken the necessary risk. Now we must, as wise men do, demonstrate a bit more patience and pray that Allah will be on our side. Let us then gather our families and go home with warm hearts and hopes for a new and better Iran."

Chapter Forty-One

Life in Paris gradually moved into a routine for both Jamie and Emma. He found himself in much more civil territory, spying largely on the French, Belgians, and Germans. The work was interesting, and even exciting on occasion, but didn't come close to the stress level he had confronted in Iran.

Emma again found herself falling in love with her first graders who, as one would expect, were a bit more sophisticated and academically advanced for their age than her students in Salmon. Given that these were largely children from the highly educated US diplomatic staff in France, academics had been pushed as soon as they were old enough to communicate. It was a different kind of challenge, and Emma loved it.

She also quickly grew to love French food. Soon after settling into her teaching routine, she signed up for a new, more advanced series of cooking lessons. The results were a joy for both her and Jamie until they began to feel some snugness in their waistlines. Having never experienced this problem before, Emma quickly adjusted portion sizes to reverse their sudden expansion.

Emma, in her new situation, had begun to push Mohammed to the back of her mind, but he suddenly reappeared one night in a dream. At one point in the dream, they were at their favorite motel and about to make love when she began to moan audibly into Jamie's ear on the pillow beside her. To him, it sounded as though she was about to experience an orgasm.

"Emma," he said as he gently shook her. She continued moaning. He shook her more firmly, and her eyes opened. Her mouth was agape. "Em, you sound like you're having fun," he said, "but I really have to get some sleep. Don't forget that I'm leaving town for a week early tomorrow morning."

"Jamie," she responded, "what just happened? Was I snoring or something?"

"No, honey, you were moaning. It sounded like a great sexual experience, but you didn't even call my name. Hope I shouldn't be jealous. Haha."

Emma was mortified. "Sorry, Jamie. I guess I must have been dreaming, but I can't remember what it was all about. Go back to sleep. I'll try to be up with you tomorrow, but if I don't make it, have a successful trip."

They both rolled over in bed, facing in opposite directions. Emma, of course, knew exactly what she had been dreaming about and was thanking God that Mo's name hadn't crossed her lips. Then she let her mind lapse back into the wonderful visual from the dream as she thought of all the sweet love from her affair with Mo. She smiled to herself, remembering those special moments and wondering how her other love was coping back in Salmon.

Emma didn't awaken in time to see Jamie off on his trip. It was Saturday, so there was no need to rush off to school. As she sipped her morning coffee, her mind wandered back to Salmon and Mo. As she gazed around the room, she saw a note on their wall calendar that Jamie's first R&R would come due at Christmas. With all the adjustments made in moving to a new country and starting new jobs and a whole new life together, Jamie's time off had slipped their minds.

She thought, *How wonderful if we could be in Salmon for Christmas…just a short week away.* At that thought, she called Jamie at the airport and had him paged before he boarded his flight. He was on board with the idea and asked her to make reservations. By the end of the day, they were booked on a direct flight to Chicago, where they would change planes for the final leg to Boise. Their parents would pick them up for the two-week vacation in Salmon.

One week later, Jamie returned from his trip. He hugged Emma, told her what he could (not much) of what he had been doing, and then got into a lively discussion of how much fun it would be at home for a couple of weeks. As they prepared for bed, the phone rang. Jamie took it in the living room. After half an hour, he came back to bed with a sour look on his face.

"What is it, honey?" asked Emma.

"Well, it's not good. You can forget everything we just talked about regarding Salmon.

We have an emergency in Saudi, and they're asking me to be at the embassy in two days. It involves the project I was working on there, and they said I should pack for a one-week stay. With all the other things on my plate, it would hardly pay to fly back to Salmon for just a couple of days, even if I was lucky enough to get a flight during the holidays."

Emma came over to him, gave him a hug and said, "Jamie, since I'll be off anyway at that time and you won't be here, would you mind if I went home to see everyone and just come back for New Year's Eve so we can spend it together?"

"I guess that would be fine. No reason to punish you for this. We can make up for it in the summer when I'll have even more R&R time accumulated. Maybe we'll take a couple of weeks to tour Europe and save the last two weeks for a trip home."

"Thanks, Jamie. Sounds like a great plan."

Once under the covers, Emma's mind wandered back home and quickly found itself focused on Mohammed. She would be there alone and staying with her parents. However, she thought, they could work out times to be alone and discuss all that had happened before she left for Paris.

Chapter Forty-Two

Stu met Jamie at the airport. As soon as they were on the road, he began to detail what had gone on since Jamie had left. When Jamie heard that after several weeks of soul-searching, Mustafa had met with Samir and agreed to make an effort to "turn" the general in charge of the Republican Guard, he was ecstatic.

"Stu, what's the timing on this?"

"Well, we're making some preliminary arrangements, which I'll get into when we get back to the embassy. Once those things are in place, Mustafa will make his initial contact with the general. I would guess that to be somewhere in the next two to four weeks."

"Wow," said Jamie, in his typically enthusiastic manner. "What a break this would be if we could make it work. I'm crossing my fingers and toes already. By the way, how is my buddy Samir doing? I know he was more than a little nervous when I was here."

"Still is, Jamie. That's the biggest reason you're here."

They had arrived at the embassy. The two of them went directly to the CIA area in the lower basement. As Stu showed Jamie to the room where he'd be staying, a familiar face came into view. It was Ken Griffin, a.k.a. Ali, his replacement in Iran.

"Hey, Ken, great to see you. Stu tells me there's been some real progress in Tehran."

"Yes, we're hoping that it all works out. If it does, it will be one of the greatest coups in the history of the CIA. I just hope you can help us keep things calm with the gentlemen you turned in our favor. Nervousness with them is truly an understatement. You'll be seeing them here in a couple of days for a planning/calming session. I'll catch you up on the details tonight."

That evening, Stu and Ken laid out the plan and tentative timing. They also explained that while it was most unusual to have contacts like Samir and Ibrahim come to the embassy, the two men indicated they wouldn't move ahead unless they could meet with the CIA agents face-to-face outside of Iran, and they wanted Jamie to be present for the meeting.

Stu said, "We told them we would arrange the next meet, but that we couldn't tell them where it would be until they were safely out of Iran."

It was now Tuesday. The plan included separate exits from Iran via different countries that could logically be explained as business travel for each man. Samir would travel first to southern Spain to ostensibly buy foodstuffs. Ibrahim, a business consultant, would fly to Qatar to see a client. Samir would then fly from Spain to Qatar, where the two men would be met by CIA agents and be driven to Riyadh. The meeting at the embassy would take place on Saturday.

Chapter Forty-Three

It was the evening of December 15 when Emma's plane landed in Boise. The Steeles and Duncans were rife with excitement as she came through the gate. In an instant, she was swarmed with hugs and kisses and endless questions about everything in Paris...especially why Jamie couldn't come home.

After doing her best to answer the questions, she just wanted a little quiet as all the familiar sights began to appear. She felt suddenly enveloped in the warmth of home, even with the snow falling all around her. She was gloriously happy!

The Steeles dropped the Duncans at their house and then drove two more blocks to their home. Emma couldn't wait to go inside. She rushed to her old room and leapt into her bed. Her parents followed close behind.

"Mom, Dad," she said, "I'm so happy and so, so jet-lagged. Would you mind if I just crawl under the covers and not move till tomorrow morning?"

"Of course not, honey," said her mom. "You sleep, and we'll see you in the morning for your favorite home-cooked breakfast. We love you. It's so wonderful to have you back!"

Twelve hours later, Emma slowly opened her eyes. Her mom had already checked in on her three times. On her fourth try, she saw her just begin to stir.

"Oh my, Emma, you weren't kidding about being tired. Think you're ready to hit the floor?"

"Oh, Mom, it feels so good in here. I hate to move. It's just like it felt when I was little." She then rolled over, put a pillow over her head, and said, "I just need another half hour. I promise I'll be in the kitchen then."

"Okay, honey. We'll be ready for you then."

After enjoying french toast, orange juice, and coffee, the expected interrogation about everything in Paris restarted. After an hour, Emma was finally able to get away to take a shower and get dressed. At 10:30 a.m., she said she was going to take a walk through town to say hello to her old friends. While this was true, there was only one old friend she had in mind. It didn't take too long to walk over to his shop. It was Monday, so she knew he would be in. Once she entered, she saw he was alone, his back to the door.

"Hi, Mo," she said spritely.

He froze, then turned very slowly to face her. His jaw dropped. He found it impossible to say a word. She saw his state of shock and decided to walk around the counter and go directly to him. She promptly pulled him behind a row of suits to block the view from the street, put her arms around him, and kissed him full on the lips. Mohammed started to respond but then stopped. He gently pushed her back and just stared at her as she smiled brightly.

"I don't know what to do," he said. "You asked me to stay away, and I respected your wishes. You can't imagine how difficult it has been. And now you appear and kiss me in a way that seems as though you had never left. You should know that I want to be with you more than anything on earth, but I can't be led down a path to nowhere. Please tell me what's going on."

As Emma was about to explain, several customers entered the shop.

"Take care of them, Mo. I'll sneak out the back. But meet me in North Fork at 1:00 for lunch so we can talk. See you then."

Emma quickly exited through the back door, leaving Mohammed to gather his faculties as he went to the front to take care of his customers. Lunch couldn't come soon enough.

Chapter Forty-Four

Saturday morning started normally for Jamie. He felt relaxed as he drank coffee with the current CIA crew and then spent an hour reading the *New York Times*. As he rose to return to his room, Stu entered the dining area and motioned for Jamie to follow him.

"They just arrived, Jamie. They're being taken to their rooms and will have a chance to shower and change before our meeting. There will be five of us at this lunch—you, me, Ken, Samir, and Ibrahim. Ken had just enough time alone with me to advise of a new wrinkle, but not enough time to explain it. So be ready for most anything."

It had been many months since Jamie had seen Samir. When he entered the conference room where lunch was to be served, Jamie was taken aback. This kind man, who had been on the plump side when he met him, must have lost fifty pounds. His once-tanned skin was significantly paler, and there were many new lines across his brow.

As soon as they made eye contact, Samir moved quickly to embrace his friend. Ibrahim, who hadn't changed as much, followed suit. Having dealt with these two for as long as he had, he knew their pent-up emotions would soon burst forth.

After waiters poured some wine to begin the luncheon, and Stu offered a toast, it became obvious that eating was to be very much an afterthought for the visitors. As they started to blurt out their *personal* concerns, Ken held up his hand to stop them.

"Gentlemen," he said, "before we get into your other request, it is really most important that we update both Stu and Jamie on the status of our plan. They must know in detail what is to happen next week."

With that, Ken went on to describe the anticipated contact of Mustafa with his dear friend, General Abdullah, the leader of the Republican Guard, in an effort to turn him to their cause. The key element in this effort would be to suggest that he become the new leader of a secular Iran. Once the mullahs were limited to religious leadership, General Abdullah would then put together a new cabinet, write a new constitution, and ultimately run for election in a reconstructed democratic society. Obviously, the key to making this work would be that his ego would be stronger than his loyalty to the existing regime. Without that, the effort would not only fail, it would surely mean death to all the conspirators and likely their families as well.

With this as a segue, Samir rose and faced Jamie. "My dear friend, it is most important that you know why we requested this meeting. Ibrahim and I and all our friends know that there is no better than a fifty-fifty chance that this plan will work. As you know, we have all agreed to accept the risk. But the two of us, as leaders of this effort, face the greatest danger if things go badly. Your country has promised to protect our families in the event of danger.

"However, we feel that things are such that if we move ahead, we want our families to leave *before* we act. That means that we must have them out of Iran by Tuesday of next week. We proposed this escape to Ken two weeks ago, and he said he had been given permission to get them out of Iran by that time with an intermediate stop in Europe until they can finalize arrangements for a permanent stay in the United States. We had hoped that all of us would go to the same place. However, there is not sufficient room in your embassy for everyone. Therefore, Ibrahim's wife, Rama, and eleven children will be staying for three months or so at the US embassy located in London. Soya and my three boys will, thankfully, be in Paris for the same period where, we were told, you are based. They will also be so happy to meet your lovely wife. Now I know you could have been informed of this through a third party, but you were the man who really provided us with this extraordinary opportunity. As we stand here, we also know that tomorrow could well be the last time we see one another. We couldn't allow things to move ahead without seeing you first."

"Wow," said Jamie. "I can't tell you how gratified I am not only by what is about to happen but by the relationship and trust that we have been able to establish. It truly seems as though we've known each other for a lifetime, not just a year and a half. My dear friends, may I commend you for your honesty and your strength in moving forward with this effort. May I also say that both Emma and I will have great joy in looking after Soya and your three young men, one of whom, I believe, is the right age to attend Emma's first grade class."

"Oh my," blurted Samir, "that's right. Abdullah just had his sixth birthday. That would be more than I could have hoped for."

With the plan in place, the two much-relieved Iranians could relax and enjoy the delicious lunch being served.

Chapter Forty-Five

Emma arrived in North Fork just before 1:00 p.m. and scanned the menu as she waited for Mo. Her now-more-refined French palate discarded the limited and very mediocre wine selections out of hand and smartly decided a cold beer would be much better with the burger she always ordered there. As she looked up from the menu, she saw Mo coming through the door. As he came to the table, she stood and gave him a friendly hug. The table she had selected at the rear of the room was far from the few people left in the restaurant, so they had the ability to talk privately. This was really a spot where most of the action happened at night. They had a decent lunch crowd, but by 1:00 in the afternoon, most all of them had left.

After the waitress took their order, Mo turned to Emma, his eyes soaking in her beauty, and his heart very much on his sleeve. "So, Em, talk to me. Have we come full circle, or is this just a tease? I've never known you to be mean-spirited, so I certainly hope it's not the latter."

"Oh, Mo," she whispered, "I would never want to hurt you in any way. You are without a doubt the kindest, gentlest man I have ever known. I just need to explain some things that I couldn't before because of both time and circumstances. Now that I've been away and have had time to think about where we were then and what has gone on since I've been away, I can tell you much more accurately about my feelings for you, my emotional situation, and what might lie in our future."

Mo sat back to listen as Emma continued. "When I agreed to go with Jamie to Paris, I didn't know what in the world had happened to you. Never before had you not been there for me. Then with almost no explanation, you had to go off with your father to solve what you called 'business problems.' Well, everyone in business occasionally has some business problems, but they generally don't become incommunicado. Just when I needed you most, you simply disappeared. And by the time you returned, so many emotions regarding my family came into play that I just didn't know what to do. So I guess I just took the easier way out. It didn't mean that I didn't still love you because I did…and I still do. That's why I came to see you. Why I had to kiss you. Why I still long to make love to you with all the sweetness and caring you've always shown."

Mo's eyes flickered at the memory of making love to Emma, how her body felt in his hands.

Emma continued speaking, "Now, don't get me wrong. Jamie and I have managed to build a life together in Paris. While he still has to travel a good deal and, of course, can't share most of what he does, we have had some good times, and he is much more thoughtful than he used to be. But the thing is, Mo, he just isn't you. So if you've been torn, you should know that I've been living a double life in my own mind and have been trying to figure out a way to bring us back together that won't destroy our families in the process."

Mo soaked in the words, trying to make sense of it all while knowing in his heart that there was no strategy that wouldn't, in some way, be hurtful. The waitress returned to the table, and the two of them began to eat in silence.

Emma put her hand on Mo's arm and asked, "Are you busy the rest of the afternoon?"

"No, Em. I had hoped to spend it with you."

"Good. I'm going to call home and tell them that I'll be home late and not to make dinner for me. Then we can sneak off to our special place and just hold each other like we used to."

Chapter Forty-Six

Orly was jammed with business travelers at eight o'clock on Tuesday morning. Jamie had a coded sign reading simply S3 (Soya and three boys) that he held aloft as the crowds were passing through customs. He was beginning to wonder if he would be able to spot them in the rush that surrounded him when suddenly, to his right, he spotted the most beautiful woman he had ever seen—jet-black hair, light brown skin, and a lithe five-foot-seven figure dressed in the latest Western style. No habit. No veil. No head covering of any kind. She was accompanied by three young boys of similar coloring dressed like young Americans on vacation in Paris.

"Assaf?" she whispered. No response. She tried again. "I'm sorry. Jamie, is it?"

"Oh my," responded Jamie as he stared somewhat agape at this incredible creature he would never have recognized. "Soya? I'm so sorry, but I've simply never seen your face before. And all of you are dressed as Westerners. I guess you'd call it hiding in plain sight. But quickly, please, come with me."

As they moved with purpose toward the exit, Soya said, "You must also remember that I have never seen you before without your full beard. Were it not for your sign, we might never have connected."

"You're right on that score," replied Jamie. "Oh, this is our car."

They entered the black GMC Denali SUV while their driver loaded the luggage. In a flash, they were off to the embassy.

When all were settled in their seats, Soya said, "I guess you must be more than a little surprised at our change to Western clothing. Now that we're out of Iran, there are some things I can share with you that might help to explain. While my parents were both Iranian, they emigrated to America a year before I was born. I grew up in San Francisco and never saw Iran until I was twenty. My father, a wonderful man who unfortunately has passed on, was somewhat Americanized but held on to a few Iranian traditions, including arranged marriages. I was a good student and finished early at Stanford. As a *graduation gift*, he brought me to Iran and announced, after we had arrived, that he had arranged my marriage. His oldest childhood friend, he said, had a son who was ready. I was shocked and upset and wanted nothing but to leave on the next plane. But for the first time in my life, my father screamed at me and said that I had no choice in the matter. It was *a fait accompli*, and he 'knew' I would grow to love the young man."

Jamie listened intently, surprised at the story he was hearing, and at Soya's forthrightness.

Soya continued, "When we went to his friend's home in Tehran, I was introduced to Samir. We were surrounded by family…hardly the way one meets a boy in the United States. While he was as sweet as can be, and I must say, much slimmer than he was when you met him, I didn't know quite what to do. This whole thing was so foreign in every way. In any event, I was stuck. I was told that after three days of getting to know each other while being escorted by relatives at every turn, we were to be married. Then came the next shocker. Father had arranged to send all my clothes and other belongings to the new home that Samir's father had purchased for us in Tehran. One thing I refused to do, however, was to give up my US citizenship. After much argument, my new father-in-law managed to bribe the right people and get me a permanent visa. As a result, my boys and I are considered US citizens, and as much as I have grown to love Samir, I am delighted to be out of that country forever!"

Jamie was astounded at what he had just heard. The boys, fortunately, hadn't paid much attention, being much more interested in how different Paris was from Tehran.

"Quite a story," Jamie finally replied. "I never would have guessed you had that kind of history, but I can certainly understand your desire to leave Iran. I'm glad for your boys too. The opportunities stateside will be much greater. And from what Samir mentioned, Abdullah is ready to enter first grade. Hopefully, he'll have Emma as his teacher. We're working on making that happen."

When they pulled up to the American embassy, the boys were in awe of the beautiful structure. When Soya told them this would be their home for the next few months, they were thrilled. Soya, too, marveled not only at her new residence but at the fact she would soon recapture the life she had once known. She hoped Samir would come through his "project" alive and well, though he had hidden from her most of the details and just how dangerous things could become.

"Well," said Jamie, "it's home sweet home for you now. The building next door is the American school where the boys will be spending much of their time. Once you're settled in, we'd love to have you all come to our home for dinner. We're just a short walk away, and Emma's become a fabulous French chef."

"I can't tell you how I look forward to it," said Soya. And in her new mind-set as an American, she stepped over to Jamie and gave him a warm hug.

Chapter Forty-Seven

It was a particularly hot day in Tehran. Many were leaving work early, especially the privileged and powerful who had swimming pools at home where they could luxuriate as most people continued to slave away. The general was on a bright green float in his pool, a subtle smile on his face as he enjoyed his status to the fullest.

His repose was unexpectedly interrupted by his housekeeper, who said, "General, your friend, the mullah Mustafa, has come to call."

"You may bring him here to the pool," he said without opening his eyes or losing his smile.

In a moment, Mustafa, wearing his full robes in the searing heat, came to the pool area. "Assalamu alaikum, my friend. I'm glad I caught you alone on this suffocating day. I must admit I am jealous of your comfort in the water."

"Ah, yes, my friend, it is with a great sense of relief that I am here. I was having a particularly difficult day with your religious compatriots this morning. There are times when I wonder just how far they will go to enforce their brand of Sharia law. Perhaps you can convince them that my main thrust is to protect the country from its enemies and that it should be the local police who enforce minor crimes."

"It is ironic, my friend," said Mustafa, "that you mention this problem. As we have discussed before, I too wonder at times about the lack of reason that my associates exhibit. It has, I might say, been an item of frequent discussion among others who rank highly in our society.

"The general attitude among many is that they are slowly destroying our country's ability to deal with the world at large. Between sanctions on the one hand and a total lack of trust among many, the problems we've been having are being exacerbated exponentially. Tell me, have you ever considered doing something definitive to change this course we're on?"

"You know, I have, but then something always seems to come up to divert my attention, and I let it slide. I guess that part of it is laziness, but I must admit that my position has allowed me a much better life than I had ever imagined I would have. However, I must say that it sounds as though you have given it more than a bit of thought. Tell me more."

"Well, my friend, you are correct. I have been giving this problem a great deal of thought. I am, after all, a very religious man who believes completely in the teachings of the Koran. However, interpretations of these teachings do vary greatly. Unfortunately, some do not believe in progress or in accepting the idea that the world has developed new ideas, created new modes of life, and no longer accepts the brutal concepts of our ancestors, such as stonings or beheadings, for what are, in a contemporary world, relatively minor offenses. I believe that we mullahs, as religious leaders, should exert our influence within the mosque in a more humane fashion and remove ourselves from day-to-day government. A secular government, I feel, with democracy as its methodology, would be the best approach for our country, led by a man not only with power but with a sense of fairness and a capacity for leadership."

"And where, may I ask, would you find such a man, Mustafa?"

"Frankly, my friend, I feel that I am looking at him right now."

Chapter Forty-Eight

Emma had returned from her trip home and temporary reinstatement of her relationship with Mo. Their relationship was rekindled but was once again on hold. They had taken full advantage of their time together to express their love for each other, both in bed and through their everyday discourse. Emma had even dared to invite Mo to her family Christmas dinner as an old friend and "stand-in" for his good buddy, Jamie. Unfortunately for them, their time passed too quickly. On her return to Paris, Emma began preparation for the new semester with Mo again left alone on the sidelines.

*****

Three weeks had now passed since the arrival of the Allem family in Paris. Soya and the boys set up their temporary residence in the embassy. With a bit of luck combined with a push from the CIA, Abdullah found his way into Emma's classroom. After spending most of her time settling the boys into their new environment with an emphasis on establishing new friendships for them, Soya now had time to readapt herself to a Western lifestyle. In truth, it came back rather easily. And with significant funds transferred from Samir's Swiss bank account, she was able to pleasure herself on Place Vendome with baubles previously verboten to her. She was quite pleased with it all, and as much as she loved Paris, she longed for the day when she could return to her beloved San Francisco and the many friendships she had left there.

When Soya returned to the embassy apartment from her shopping trip, she found a message from Emma inviting her and the boys to dinner on Saturday just two days away. She called Emma immediately and happily accepted the invitation, promising to bring a very special champagne to celebrate her new life in the West.

The days passed quickly, and she soon found herself and the boys crammed into the small elevator that slowly climbed the four stories to the Duncans' apartment. The aromas coming from the kitchen were enticing. The boys, in particular, had been having a difficult time adjusting to French cuisine but were getting the hang of it and beginning to enjoy it. The adjustment began with pastries, followed by the joy of sweet butter on warm French baguettes. And now, with Emma's new expertise in French cuisine, their appreciation for these fine new flavors grew further. Emma had sensed that she should not make something too exotic for the sake of the boys. A wise decision on the part of the schoolteacher who had been watching Abdullah grow into his new lifestyle on a daily basis.

The Taittinger Blanc de Blanc was exquisite. Emma, Jamie, and Soya toasted everything they could think of before their dinner of duck a l'orange (for the adults) and fried chicken for the boys began. There was also one "silent" toast by Emma to Mo, as he never left her thoughts for long.

The evening passed quickly, and at 8:00 p.m., Soya noticed the boys were beginning to tire. Jamie said that although the embassy was nearby, he thought it would be wise to walk them home for safety reasons. Soya thanked him and accepted the offer. The three adults cleared the table, leaving Emma with a small mountain of dishes. With hugs and kisses all around, Jamie, Soya, and the boys left.

*****

Jamie put Soya and the boys in the elevator and quickly descended the stairs to meet them at the ground floor. As Soya left the elevator, Jamie could hardly avoid looking at her in a way he couldn't upstairs. She was truly exquisite, not to mention brilliant. And now that he knew her beyond her reserved manner in Iran, he was becoming increasingly attracted to this very worldly woman.

Conversation on the way home was casual, with the boys straggling a bit as they tired further. Soya began to express some concern over Samir's safety, which Jamie tried to calm by saying that the people he was working with were very talented and that their cause was certainly just. He wouldn't go into more detail, and of course, he couldn't know exactly how much Samir might have shared with her.

When they arrived at the embassy, Soya sent the boys inside and then turned to Jamie. "Thank you, Jamie, my friend, for all you have done for us. This evening, as well, was such a special bonus. I only hope that someday we will be able to repay you."

With this, she stepped forward and gave Jamie a warm hug, kissed his cheek, and left without another word.

Quite a night, thought Jamie, with a whole new train of thought racing through his mind.

Chapter Forty-Nine

Mustafa ended up spending three more hours with the general. After leaving the pool and showering, the man with whom he was placing his very strong hopes emerged in relaxed dress and suggested that Mustafa stay for an early dinner. They discussed in detail Mustafa's thoughts of how he envisioned an enlightened democracy in Iran, how it might be created, what obstacles might be encountered with the mullahs, and whether he could conceive of Khomeini giving up his absolute power over everything in the country in exchange for control only of the religious side of things.

In response, the general concerned himself with himself. He knew he had control of the military and could *force* the mullahs to accept a lesser role. His greater concern was whether Mustafa truly believed that he had the ability and political and intellectual know-how to lead the country into becoming a secular state and whether he could properly manage that state after it was established.

Mustafa, of course, could do nothing but support the idea, strongly massaging the general's ego with every word.

By the time he left, Mustafa felt there was a good chance he had convinced his friend to move ahead. And aside from the egotistical side of the ledger, there was the side of common sense. Other than Khomeini and his small group of yes men, most of the country yearned for the changes they had just discussed.

"My dear Mustafa," said the general, "I must now give serious consideration to all we have talked over. As you know, this would be no small endeavor. I will promise you only one thing…that I will review every aspect carefully and get back to you as soon as I have made a decision. In the meantime, neither of us should speak a word of this until we meet again."

With that, the two men embraced, and Mustafa headed to the mosque for evening prayer.

Chapter Fifty

Mustafa contacted Samir and suggested they meet immediately with Ali and Ibrahim to review his meeting with
the general. The meeting was arranged for the following
day and took place in the same guesthouse they had used
previously. When Mustafa related the details, the men were
both thrilled with the possibilities and, at the same time,
very much on edge. Which way would he go, and how
would it affect them? All that Samir and Ibrahim knew for
sure was that they were so glad their families had made a
safe exit from Iran.

Ali tried to keep the tensions down within the group,
stressing to Mustafa that he couldn't push too quickly for
an answer. He emphasized that when it came down to it,
the general was going to realize there was much more than
an ego trip involved here and that his self-admitted ten-
dency toward "laziness"—or perhaps fear of the enormity
of the project—could again come into play and cause a
serious problem.

"Give him some time to consider it but not enough
time to talk himself out of it and take the lazy path. That
path would not lead to a good place for any of us."

The meeting ended, and three of the men went home with their private thoughts. Ken headed back to Saudi to review the situation with Stu.

Chapter Fifty-One

Jamie had a lunch meeting at a small bistro near the Louvre. As he finished his business, he decided to spend a couple of hours looking at the art he had not previously had time to see since his arrival in the country. The afternoon was balmy, the air clear, and he felt relaxed as he entered the glass pyramid that served as an entrance. As he stepped on the escalator, he felt a hand tap gently on his shoulder. He turned to find a smiling Soya looking back at him.

"Well," she said, "what a surprise. What brings you here at this time of day?"

"I just finished some business nearby and decided it was high time I get a little culture in my life."

"Aha," she replied. "My thoughts exactly. I really haven't seen much art since I moved to Iran. When Samir and I visited the States, we did spend some time at the Met in New York. When I was at Stanford, I would occasionally spend time at the de Young Museum in San Francisco. But now I have a feast of art at my fingertips, so I will not let this precious time in Paris be wasted. Last week I was at L'Orangerie, and this week, I start my tour of the Louvre. Please join me. It would be much more fun to see it with a friend."

"I couldn't agree more," said Jamie. "Seeing the Mona Lisa with a beautiful woman would be a delight indeed."

As they walked toward the room where this most visited piece of art was housed, Jamie suddenly found himself talking like he was still single and back in school. There was always a "wise-ass" remark that came as a natural instinct to him. And regardless of the nature of the woman he was with, he invariably made it work. After all, Jamie Duncan was an exceptionally bright and engaging young man. However, he was quite human and subject to the yearnings that every healthy young man has. In the long months he had spent away from Emma, his fidelity had failed him on at least a dozen occasions. None of these were affairs, just one-night stands with girls he had met in bars along the way. Soya offered the potential of a totally different experience. He surely didn't know how or if he could make this incredibly strong yearning become a reality. He just knew it might be worth the effort. Jamie pushed down all thoughts of betrayal to Emma and Samir as his hormones began to roar. Ethics, with regard to women in his life, sometimes just got in the way.

"There it is," said Soya excitedly. "Oh my, it seems so small. I always thought of it as a larger canvas."

They tried to get close, but the room was extraordinarily crowded. After waiting a while, they made it to the front of the crowd only to have Jamie remark, "I must say that after all this, I'm disappointed. I would much rather spend my time here with the likes of Renoir, Monet, and Sargent."

"You know," replied Soya, "I couldn't agree more. Let's find them."

What Jamie was intending to be a visit of an hour or two turned into four. The chatter was nonstop as they found their opinions on the very subjective area of fine art running along the same plane. Here were two good-looking, intelligent, and worldly people quickly creating a special bond.

When the museum was about to close, Soya suggested they stop for a glass of wine before heading home. She said her boys were having a sleepover with some new friends, so she had one of her first free evenings in ages. Emma was engaged with parents' night and wouldn't be home until 9:00 that evening. She and Soya had been in touch on a regular basis regarding Abdullah's progress, so Emma had already given her all the information the other parents would be receiving that evening.

"Tell you what," said Jamie, "let me go one better and buy you dinner. There's a great little place I've grown to love in the 7th Arrondissement that you really should get to know. Let's grab a taxi and head over there."

As usual, the traffic was brutal, but twenty minutes later, they were ensconced in a booth at a very cozy, dimly lit restaurant. Their talk and wine and food, and more wine went on for hours. When Jamie finally excused himself to use the restroom, he looked at his watch to see it was already half past nine. *Better get home before Emma becomes concerned*, he reasoned in his wine-driven haze.

He and Soya left the restaurant and quickly hailed another taxi. At this late hour, they were back at the embassy in just thirty minutes. Jamie decided he would walk home from there. As he and Soya reached the door of the embassy, he stared straight into her eyes. She held his gaze for a long moment, not wanting the evening to end. Finally, and probably because guilt began to creep into their two psyches, they hugged, exchanged cheek kisses, and said a longing good night.

As Jamie headed home, he saw a familiar figure step out from the school and onto the sidewalk. She was walking in the same direction. Before he caught up to Emma, he had the presence of mind to rub clean the cheek where Soya had planted her goodbye kiss. He ran very quietly and wrapped his arms around Emma from behind, scaring her into a shrill scream that must have been heard throughout the neighborhood.

"Emma," he said, "quiet down. It's just me."

"Oh my god, Jamie, you scared the hell out of me. And why are you out here on the street at this late hour?"

Jamie went on to relate the story of meeting Soya at the museum, keeping it all at a very platonic level. As soon as he finished—and to change the subject—he said, "And I thought you were going to be home by nine this evening."

"I know," she replied, "but each of these high-end parents thinks that theirs is the only child in the world and wants to know every detail of their life in school as if they didn't hear about it every day when their kids were doing homework. And by the way, just how much wine did you and the beautiful Soya consume? You smell like you just came from an all-day wine tasting."

"Well, I must admit we did manage two bottles. She needed some local knowledge of the food and wine scene, so I agreed to help."

"Sounds just like you, Jamie Duncan!"

Chapter Fifty-Two

The four weeks that had passed seemed like four years to the group of friends awaiting the general's response. Ken decided to call another meeting. Back in Samir's guest-house, the looks on their faces were fraught with worry. Mustafa was the last to arrive.

After a few social words with his friends, Mustafa cast his gaze on Ken, who quickly called the meeting to order. "Gentlemen," he began, "we have now waited four long weeks without a word from the man who controls not only the Republican Guard but, indirectly, the lives of every man in this room. My personal feeling is that Mustafa must make contact to at least see the direction in which the general might be leaning. Do the rest of you agree or have any other thoughts?"

No one spoke up. They just looked to Mustafa for guidance. After a long pause, the mullah spoke, "Ali is right. By now, if he is serious, he should have some idea. If he has fallen to his lazy ways, we may as well know now. I will call on him this evening."

*****

At 8:00 p.m., Mustafa came to the general's door unannounced. The servant, who knew him well, answered the ring and welcomed Mustafa in. "Please wait here," he said, "the general is just finishing dinner."

He soon returned and asked Mustafa to follow him to the library. The general embraced his friend, asked him to sit, and looked—no, glared—at him for several seconds. Then he spoke.

"My dear friend," he said, "a month or so ago we spoke at length of your interest in a governmental change. You suggested some intriguing ideas, many of which I wholeheartedly agree with. You spoke of my using the power of the Republican Guard to carry out this venture and of my becoming the new leader of our country. All this was, I admit, quite appealing. In fact, until just a few hours ago, I was ready to call you and set things in motion."

The general paced the floor and paused before continuing. "However, at 10:00 this morning, I received a disturbing message. I must admit that it shook me to my core, especially because you were the key person involved. You see, we have been suspicious of a few people and have been trying to gain information about them. We suspected an American plan but had no firm evidence until today. It seems a servant of your friend, Samir Allem, overheard a suspicious discussion that took place just before you came to see me on this topic. He had been trying to report the situation to the authorities, but being a low-level individual, the police didn't pay attention to him. Finally, he came directly to my headquarters building swearing that his message was urgent. My men were about to throw him out on the street when I heard him shout your name. I took him into my office, and he told me of a plot that matched closely with our discussion. He also said that a man calling himself Ali had a strange accent, and he believed that he was not an Iranian. Yesterday, we found Ali and found that he was, in fact, living in a safe house…a US safe house. He is now in custody. And as we speak, Samir, Ibrahim, and the rest of your boyhood friends are being arrested. You understand, of course, that it will be necessary for you to be punished along with your friends. However, since I cannot be implicated in this matter, we will have to handle your situation a bit differently. Please come with me."

Mustafa knew this was his end. There would be no escaping the general. It was just a matter of when and how. Those questions were soon to be answered.

Mustafa and the general entered the back seat of his limousine. Without a word, the driver drove into the desert. In a desolate area behind a large dune, he stopped the car. The driver opened the door for Mustafa while the general got out on the other side. About twenty yards from the car, Mustafa could see a large hole in the ground. The driver moved him there and faced him toward the hole. He then calmly drew his pistol, placed it at the back of Mustafa's head, and fired. Mustafa's body fell forward into the grave. The driver then holstered his gun. As he did so, another shot rang out. The driver fell on top of Mustafa. The general then took a shovel from the trunk of his car and covered their bodies. Mustafa's mysterious disappearance was never mentioned again.

The twelve friends were now in twelve isolation cells. Each day, one of them would be taken out and tortured. Each day, the screams of that friend would be heard by all the others.

When the police had finally wrung every bit of information out of the men, they were marched with great ceremony to an area of the prison where the public could watch executions. A large gallows had been constructed so that all twelve men could be hung at the same moment. The mullahs had given the execution great publicity, highlighting in excruciating details the conspiracy these men had created with the Great Satan.

When the moment came, the men were marched to the gallows and blindfolded. Samir and Ibrahim stood next to each other. The nooses were placed around their necks. The trap doors fell!

To be sure the public understood the full measure of pain that would come to them if they were to attempt such an act of treason, the wives and children of the rest of the men were marched to a concrete wall adjacent to the gallows. Ten women and forty-three children stood there sobbing. Five men, their heads covered in ski masks, stepped forward with machine guns at the ready. Upon a signal from the prison warden, fifty-three lives ended in just seconds.

Chapter Fifty-Three

The day before the men were arrested, Jamie left on a top-secret mission for three weeks. He was completely isolated from the world when this atrocity took place. When he returned to the embassy, everyone stared at him with a strange look and then avoided further eye contact. When he entered his office, he found Stu sitting across from his chair.

"Hey, Stu!" he shouted. "What are you doing here, and why all the glum faces?"

"Have a seat, Jamie. You're not going to like what I have to say."

"What is it, Stu? What gives?"

"Your friends Samir and Ibrahim and the rest of their crew are dead!"

"Oh my god. What happened? And what about Ken?"

"He's still alive but only because they want to have a prisoner exchange. The president hasn't decided on that yet, but you know our policy."

"I do, but tell me what happened! How did they catch them?"

"Well, we're not completely sure. Could be that Mustafa screwed them over, but we don't think so because he has suddenly disappeared, and no one seems to have any idea where. It probably was the general of the Republican Guard that Mustafa was trying to turn. If he decided to cover his ass, the best thing for him to do would be to erase evidence permanently."

"Stu, does Soya know?"

"Of course. It was in all the papers. She's been a wreck, as has Ibrahim's wife, Rama, in London. While they are, of course, grateful that they and their children are alive, they also realize that their lives will never be the same."

It was already late in the afternoon when Jamie received the news. Emma would be home from school by now, and he felt sure she would be the one Soya would run to first in her sorrow.

He was right. As soon as he entered their apartment, Emma ran to him, wrapped her arms around him, and squeezed—hard!

"Oh, Jamie!" she cried. "It could have been you! It could have been you! Poor Soya. She and the boys have been in mourning for weeks. She told me everything. And now they still have one of your men as a prisoner. You must know him."

"I'm afraid I do. Ken Griffin, a good man, the same man who took over my job. This was the deal I set in motion, babe. The one that got me promoted here. I just wish I knew what happened. There had to be a leak from someplace along the line, but it sure wouldn't have been from one of those twelve men. I don't think it would have been the mullah they were turning either. It had to be something incidental, something overheard. I know they were always so concerned about people listening to their conversations. It could have been one of the servants. Tell me, have you been 'consoler in charge?'"

"I'm afraid so. I feel so bad for her…for all of them."

"Well, I hope they let them stay here at least until the school term is over, and then get them back to the States. The further away they are from all this, the better off they'll be. I guess I should make a point of seeing Soya right away. I sure hope she doesn't blame me. After all, I was the one who gave birth to all this."

Chapter Fifty-Four

Jamie arrived at his office at 6:00 a.m. the following morning so he could catch up with the paperwork that had piled up on his desk over the weeks he had been gone. By 10:00 a.m., he had the most urgent matters in hand and decided to venture up to Soya's apartment in the embassy.

He knocked on the door without response. He tried a second time and heard a subdued, "I'm coming." When the door opened, she looked at Jamie, and the tears began to flow. He thought she was going to collapse, so he reached out for her and held her close to him. Her sobs came like a torrent as she placed her arms around his neck and held on for dear life.

They stood in the doorway a full five minutes before she finally composed herself and let him into the apartment. It was the first time he had actually been in her quarters since the day they first arrived. He could see she had changed the decor on her own to make it seem more like a real home for the boys.

They began to talk, but Soya quickly took over the conversation and began to relay the nightmare from her perspective. She also talked of Rama, who was now in a bad mental state. The best thing she said was that Ibrahim's family had word they would be leaving for the States the next month, but they didn't know where exactly home would be. She then asked Jamie if he could find out what sort of schedule she and boys might be on. She wanted Abdullah to finish his school term while in Paris. It would be easier for the younger ones if they started fresh in their new home stateside.

Jamie said he would ask the question but doubted they would tell him because of the highly secretive nature of these placements. Then Jamie asked her, "Is there anything else I can do for you? Anything at all?"

"Yes, Jamie, just be my friend. I think I'll need your strength to get me through all this."

"Soya," he responded, "my friendship is something I can promise you'll always have."

Chapter Fifty-Five

The magical moment had occurred when Emma had returned home and reenergized Mohammed. Their evening at the motel had brought back all the warmth, caring, and deep love they had previously shared. Somehow, Mo thought they would find a way to return to the life they had envisioned together when Emma and Jamie next made their R&R trip back to Salmon. Now Mo would have time to work out a plan with a rationale that Emma could live with before then. He became completely involved in the details because he didn't have Emma. When she had left, she reinstated—regretfully—her rules on communication. She simply couldn't live with the threat of being caught in their affair. So their lives went on with large doses of anticipation, loneliness, and confusion.

In the meantime, Mo's father suffered a serious heart attack and, under his doctor's orders, agreed to retire. Now with full control of the business, Mohammed expanded it to several more towns, built a larger central plant facility that could service all their retail outlets, and as somewhat of a lark for a now-successful businessman, started a bungee jumping concession in his home town. Mo had tried jumping once and fell in love with it, thinking it not only exciting but also a way to make extra money with minimal investment. The town gave him permission to use the bridge on the main road leading to Salmon for all summer weekends, weather permitting. He could also use the bridge at other times for private parties or special events. It all became quite a hit with the youth of Salmon and for many tourists in the area. Mo just seemed to have the golden touch when it came to business.

As he worked on his plan to bring Emma back into his life on a permanent basis, a nasty thought came to him. It wasn't the kind of thing Mohammed—by nature, a soft, honest, peaceful sort—would normally have allowed to cross his mind. But things had become desperate, so he wasn't about to take any ideas off the table. He was sitting in his office. Through his window, he had a clear view of the bridge. At that precise moment, he could see a customer making his leap into space. What if, he thought, that was Jamie, and maybe, just maybe, something were to go wrong? An accident. With an accident, there would be no need for explanations. The families would be sad, but they would eventually get past it. After all, Jamie was a man in a profession where high risk was an everyday part of the game.

Then Mo snapped out of it. "Are you crazy?" he said to himself. "I know I'm jealous, but that would mean murder. I couldn't do that to anyone, least of all my oldest friend. It might be very convenient, but I could never live with myself afterward. I must find a better way."

Chapter Fifty-Six

Jamie, Soya, and the boys had just left Paris on the Chunnel bound for London. There was to be a private farewell party for Rama and for her and Ibrahim's children at the embassy. Soya hadn't seen her since Iran and was anxious to say goodbye to her dear friend before she left.

A private room on the top floor of the embassy building had been reserved. While the wounds of the travesty still ached, time had begun its healing process. When Soya entered the room and saw the family, she first broke into a smile followed by a rush of tears. She ran to her friend, Rama, and embraced her, then did the same to each of the children. After that, she took Rama aside for a long chat. Among other things, she wanted to find out the plan for where she would be living, what her new name would be, etc. Unfortunately, all that information was still secret. All Rama knew was that they would be the only passengers (along with two FBI agents) aboard a government jet. They had told her that once the plane was aloft, she would be given a full explanation of the plan, along with all necessary passports and related paperwork.

"Find out," said Soya, "how we can stay in touch once we've all made it over there. I'll ask the same. It will be so important for us to have each other."

"I know, my dear, I will do what I can. And thank you for all your support during this horror."

With this, the two women returned to the small group assembled in the room. At that instant, Jamie came and introduced himself to Rama, whom he had never had a chance to meet in Iran. They exchanged pleasantries, which pleased him, as he wasn't sure how she would react to the man who had started it all. As it turned out, Soya had put in many good words on his behalf during her Paris-to-London phone calls with this sweet woman. All seemed under control.

After a beautiful luncheon was served, a commemorative cake was cut. The children made short work of it, and then Stu, who had come in for the occasion, clinked a spoon against his glass to call the group to order. He spoke a few heartfelt and sobering words:

"Ladies and gentlemen, we are here today for several reasons: to honor a very brave man, to mourn his passing under the most difficult of circumstances, and to cheer his wonderful family on to a wonderful life in the States, with endless possibilities for everyone. If people like Ibrahim didn't have the courage to stand up for what is right in this world, we would all be in serious trouble. He and his compatriots risked everything and, unfortunately, lost this round. But it almost worked, and it was only the first round. There will be more. However, what is most important to say here today is a thought for Ibrahim's children. Remember, each one of you, the kind of man you had as your father. As you grow and move on in this world, he is the kind of person you want to emulate. Kind, courageous, loving, and genuine. He provided the right kind of model for you to follow. Finally, let me thank you as a family for all you have done in advancing our mutual efforts to make Iran a better country. Assalamu alaikum."

For a moment, the room remained silent as everyone absorbed Stu's wise words.

Then suddenly, the door opened, and two FBI agents entered the room and announced that all bags had been stowed on the bus and they were to leave at once for the military airport about an hour and a half away from the embassy.

It was hugs and kisses once more as Soya and Rama said their last good-byes, not knowing when or if they would ever see each other again.

Chapter Fifty-Seven

The ride back to Paris was quiet. It seemed that everyone, even Soya's young boys, were absorbed in personal
thoughts. As Jamie stared out the window of the train, he
suddenly felt a hand come quietly to rest on his. At first,
he didn't know quite how to respond. After a few minutes,
however, he turned his head enough that he could see Soya
looking at his hand in a somewhat mindless way, gently
caressing it. He really couldn't tell if she was thinking of
him or of something else with the contact being nothing
but incidental. He watched her for a few moments more
and finally said to her, "What are you thinking about?"

Without looking away from his hand, she responded,
"I've had so many thoughts on this ride that I wouldn't
know quite where to start. But at this exact moment, I
was thinking about what beautiful hands you have. Large,
strong, very manly."

"Well, thank you, I guess. I can't say that I've ever given
my own hands that much thought before."

"Well, perhaps you should. A man's hands can reveal
a lot about him. For example, why did you just happen to
win the heart of the most beautiful girl in your class? I'm
sure every other boy would have wanted Emma as his own
sweetheart."

"On that score, you're surely correct. And when you move from a big town like Chicago to a tiny spot like Salmon, you realize that you have to be sure to get the pick of the much smaller litter available."

"So are you two planning to start a family someday?"

Jamie was slow to respond.

"Did I step beyond my bounds?" asked Soya. "I hope I didn't say the wrong thing."

"No, it's not your fault. Unfortunately, Emma had a bad miscarriage that cost us big-time. She's no longer able to have children."

"I'm so sorry for you, Jamie."

"Thanks, but I have to admit that it was partially my fault." He then went on to describe what had happened while he was away at CIA camp. "She always says she's forgiven me, but I'm not completely sure. Anyway, there's nothing I can do about it now. Sometimes I look at your three boys and wish they could be mine. Guess I really do miss the idea of parenthood."

Soya took his arm and then leaned her head against his shoulder. "I understand," she said softly. "It's a wonderful feeling of joy impossible to replace in any way." She stayed in that position for the longest time, and Jamie found himself enjoying every moment.

He thought, *Am I crazy to even allow myself to have romantic feelings toward this woman? All the others were cheap one-night stands. No emotion. No danger. But this... this could be real danger. Here I have Emma, a great wife who has put up with my wild and crazy career, my ignorance in not calling her when all she wanted was to hear from me during her pregnancy after she was kind enough to agree to let me take this job. I know that she would be working on our second kid today if I hadn't taken all that away from her. And now I find myself getting carried away with thoughts of the extraordinary Soya who, as far as I know, probably has nothing but platonic thoughts of me. Not only that, Emma has become her one and only friend in Paris. Yes, I have to be crazy...I guess.*

By the time the Chunnel came to rest in Paris, the boys had fallen sound asleep, as had their mother. Jamie woke his little crew, picked up the littlest one, and hauled them to the taxi stand. At the door to the apartment, Soya turned her key in the lock, put Abdullah in charge of getting his brothers to bed, and then turned to Jamie. "It seems that every time I see you, I'm thanking you for something, this time for getting us there and back. It reminds me each time of when Samir would confide in me that he just sensed you were a man who could be trusted, that you would always be a true friend."

Soya came close this time and kissed him lightly on the lips. "Thanks," she said and quietly retreated into the apartment.

Jamie just stood still as the door closed. He felt like a man who was walking in opposite directions at the same time, going nowhere fast.

Chapter Fifty-Eight

It wasn't the first time Emma had thought about Jamie and Soya spending time together. There was always, it seemed, a legitimate reason, such as the trip to London. Yet even with her new and ongoing friendship with Soya, a small seed of suspicion seemed to linger. Each time she caught herself thinking about it, her own sense of guilt tended to bring her up short. And then there was the irony of it all. Here she was, having accusatory thoughts about her husband, possibly having romantic feelings for this Iranian woman when she, herself, had had much more than just romantic *thoughts* of an Iranian man. *Are my suspicions actually true?* she thought.

These thoughts wouldn't leave her mind. And just as she was thinking about it all, she heard Jamie come in from his trip to London. She was in bed with an unread book in her lap when he opened the bedroom door.

"Hi, babe," he said in a very tired fashion. "This was not an easy day. I'm so glad it's over."

"Did you have a chance to meet Ibrahim's wife?" she queried.

"I did. Nice lady. You could see the sorrow had hardly left her. But there was no resentment toward me. She was very kind."

"I'm glad, honey. I know that thoughts of her casting blame in your direction have been weighing on your mind for a long time. How did Soya and the boys deal with it?"

"Well, the boys are really too young to absorb everything although Abdullah did seem to pay some attention. Most of Ibrahim's kids are older, so they really had a sense of loss with their father. I have to give credit to Stu for making a short but poignant speech that I think helped to put things into perspective for them."

Jamie came close to give Emma a kiss good night. As he did so, she noticed a reddish stain on his lips. As he made contact with her, she seemed to suddenly freeze.

"You okay, Em?" he asked.

"Oh, oh, yes," she stumbled. "Must have been a nervous tick or something." Jamie didn't think much of it until he entered the bathroom to wash up before bed.

He looked in the mirror and froze. *Nervous tick, my eye*, he thought to himself. *Now I've really put my foot in it…except I really didn't do a thing.*

Chapter Fifty-Nine

Back at the US embassy in Riyadh, Stu and Ambassador Chuck Crowley were reviewing newly received information regarding the still-mysterious charitable organization known only as IGO. The FBI had gotten permission from the FISA court—which oversees surveillance warrants—to tap phone lines in the town of Salmon, Idaho. The name of an older gentleman named Ali Hassan, who had immigrated from Canada a few years back, had been mentioned several times. His background was quietly vetted, and nothing damaging had been found. As far as the FBI could tell, he operated as an independent business consultant, had only positive reviews from clients, and had never run afoul of the law. His closest friend was a man named Ali Amsur, a local businessman, recently retired, who was also of excellent repute. Yet he was their one and only lead. They wondered aloud if it was an issue worth pursuing with so many bigger fish to fry.

Finally, Stu said, "I remember discussing potential contacts in Idaho with Jamie Duncan. He came from Idaho. Maybe I should just shake the sheets up there in Paris and see if our boy recognizes the name. Anyway, it's worth a phone call."

The next day, Stu touched base with Jamie while the latter man was on a field operation. Jamie couldn't talk long, but when Stu mentioned the name Ali Hassan, he jumped.

"Yeah, Stu, I do know him, though not very well. I can ask around back home and see if there are any nibbles, though it would seem unlikely. The handful of Iranians in Salmon have always seemed too happy and grateful to be citizens to be involved in any anti-American plots. If I get anything at all on this, I'll get right back to you."

"Thanks, Jamie. Let me know either way, will you?"

"Sure thing. Whoa, gotta go now. We're breaking into a home with guns blazing, and I thought Brussels would be a quiet town. I'll be in touch."

Stu came back to Chuck's office to tell him of the conversation with Jamie. "You know, Chuck, I think our boy Jamie really loves the action. He was just handling a full-fire break-in and sounded more like Wyatt Earp kicking ass at the OK Corral."

Chapter Sixty

Mo picked up his phone. It seldom rang unless it was his father, but he knew his dad was home in bed. He was shocked when he heard Jamie's voice boom out. "Hey, you old cocksucker, you just sitting there counting the day's receipts or still up there in North Fork trying to get laid?"

It was a good thing Jamie couldn't see Mo at that moment. Mohammed used to expect greetings like that from his high school buddy, but given how Mo's life with Emma had evolved, the words didn't exactly rub quite the same way. He gathered himself.

"Hello, my man. It seems nothing has changed. You call me from out of the blue and from God knows where. It's just like you caught up with me walking home from school. How are you, and why the call at this late hour?"

"Well, I'm just great! I'm calling you from the greatest city in the world, except, of course, for Salmon. I just had a question for you. You know your dad's good buddy Ali Hassan's name came up over here. Do you, by any chance, know if he's involved with some charity organization called IGO?"

Mohammed nearly fell out of his chair. His breath shortened to quick gasps as he clung to the edge of his desk to maintain his balance. Finally, he responded, "Gee,

Jamie, I really don't know. All I really do know about the professional side of his life is that he's a business consultant. Why do you ask?"

"Well, Mo, I don't really know the details of what this outfit is all about, but there was some interest in him, and since they know I came from Salmon, they asked me to check it out. Anyway, maybe you could ask him or, even better, your dad to see if they know anything about this IGO outfit. You have my number at the embassy. Give me a call back in the next couple of days even if you don't hear anything concrete."

"I sure will, Jamie. Let me do some checking, and I'll be back to you ASAP."

"Thanks, pal." Jamie hung up.

Mo sat stunned for a while, not really knowing what to do next. His father was still in fragile health, and he worried that this kind of inquiry could kill him. He also knew Ali Hassan was on vacation for another week. He would just have to wait until he returned.

Chapter Sixty-One

Jamie knocked on Soya's apartment door. She answered and smiled broadly when she saw who it was.

"And to what do I owe this honor, Jamie?"

"It seems you owe it to some good news for you. There happen to be two gentlemen from the FBI who would like to have words with you in my office. Beyond that, I can give you no details except that you can probably make some positive assumptions."

"Oh my!" she squealed with delight. "They must have my date for going back to the States. Just let me put on some shoes and some lipstick and grab my purse. Be with you in an instant."

A minute later, they were in the elevator. Soya was so excited that she grabbed Jamie's hand and squeezed hard as she openly displayed her excitement at the idea of leaving for the States. They stepped from the elevator, which was just a short distance from Jamie's office. As they entered, the two agents rose from their chairs and greeted Soya with broad smiles. After introductions, they asked Jamie to leave as all business regarding her relocation was to be kept confidential. As things turned out, Soya and the boys were scheduled to leave in June, immediately after the school term ended. It couldn't have been more perfect. There was a raft of paperwork for Soya to sign as passports, new home, bank accounts, home location, school, etc. had to be prepared to absorb this soon-to-be "reborn" family into the States. And while Soya was fortunate to be financially sound, for now, even Samir's significant savings wouldn't last forever. She asked the agents if she would be offered a job. She reminded them that she had a degree from Stanford and would be interested in a career in finance. They said they could not make any promises but would advise the people in Washington making the arrangements.

"When you're aboard your flight back to the States, there will be more papers to sign," said Agent Johnson. "At that time, we will fill you in on all the important details and hopefully will have something for you in the way of a job prospect."

When the meeting concluded, Soya was tired but filled with hope for her future. As she and the agents left Jamie's office, he was standing outside anxiously waiting to regain his space. After cordial goodbyes to the agents, Soya came up to Jamie and again expressed her gratitude for all his help.

"Well," he said, "you're just a couple of months away from getting your wish. As I think of all that's gone on, it's hard to believe how far you've come. Let's just hope that it will be blue skies and sunshine from now on."

Jamie watched as Soya left to tell the boys the good news. As he did, he wondered to himself if two months from then would be the last he would see of her.

Chapter Sixty-Two

Emma had quietly been making plans for the four weeks of R&R Jamie had coming. As soon as the school term ended, she wanted to see as much of France as possible. Her thought was to start with the short drive to Reims to study the bubbly and eat fine food, then to move on to Beaune to sample the world's finest burgundies. From there, they would head to Lyon to visit Paul Bocuse's world-famous restaurant L'Auberge du Pont de Collonges. Then, in sequence, to Aix-en-Provence, a side trip to Monte Carlo, a night in the romantic little village of Èze, Marseilles, Bordeaux, Normandy, and back to Paris. It sounded like a lot to cram into two weeks—and it was. When Emma finally showed her plan to Jamie, he asked, "Are we spending the entire month in France? Or are we still planning on two weeks in Salmon?"

Emma blushed. "Well, maybe I have gotten a little carried away. Maybe we should just rent a car instead of using ours, drop it off in Marseilles, fly back to Orly, and connect to the States?"

"Now I think you have the right idea," said Jamie. "Why don't you go ahead and book those reservations now so we'll be set? Can't wait, and by the way, I found out today that Soya and the boys will be leaving in June. That's still on the QT."

That night, after Jamie was sound asleep, Emma decided it was time to write to Mo. She could give him the dates when she expected to be in Salmon and her thoughts of how, if they were lucky, they might have some private time together. In recent weeks, with her suspicions regarding Jamie and Soya growing, she found her thoughts of Mo getting stronger by the day. However, now that she knew Soya would be leaving soon, she would just have to see how things truly developed.

Chapter Sixty-Three

The moment Ali Hassan returned from vacation, Mohammed appeared at his front door. When he opened the door and saw the look of terror on Mo's face, he urged him to come in and have a cup of tea.

"What is it, my boy?" he offered. "You look like you've seen a ghost."

"I may as well have, Ali. Maybe three of them—yours, mine, and my dad's. I'm afraid the CIA is on our trail. You remember my best friend, Jamie Duncan, do you not?"

"Of course I do. Isn't he doing something over in Europe these days?"

"Indeed he is. For the CIA. He and Emma are stationed there now. I hadn't talked to him for some time, but while you were away, about a week ago, he called me out of the blue. He said the government had been suspicious of a group called IGO, which they thought might be based in Salmon. He didn't give me details, but they apparently had been tapping the phones, and your name had come up. So he asked me if I knew anything about IGO and if I knew if you had an association with the group."

"Well, what did you say to him?"

"I said I knew nothing of the group but that I would check with you. He asked me to let him know your answer

THE CUT ABOVE

no matter what it was. One other thing, before Jamie was assigned to Paris, he was in Saudi Arabia. That means he could have been spying on Iran. Who knows?"

"Mohammed, does your father know this?"

"No, Ali. I was afraid it could affect his heart. Please let's keep this between us."

"Okay, my boy. I agree. But let's consider your response. First, did he give you a time by which you must get back to him?"

"Not exactly…he just said to call him back either way. However, knowing Jamie, I would say the time is up right now."

"Then you should respond immediately. Simply say that you spoke with me and that I knew nothing of this group. We simply have to do what President Nixon once tried to do—stonewall it. If they know something, they'll keep pushing. If not, they're more likely to drop it altogether. We just can't open the window even one crack. Do you understand?"

"Of course, Ali. I will call him as soon as his office in Paris opens for business."

*****

When Jamie answered his phone, he said, "I thought you had forgotten about me, Mo. I was just about to call you."

"Thanks for waiting, Jamie. Turns out Ali was on vacation, so I had to wait for his return. When I asked him about IGO, he said he has no knowledge of it. So as far as

201

I can tell, it seems to end there. If I should hear something more in the future, I'll be sure to let you know."

"Well, thanks, pal. I'll let my people know what your man had to say. Gotta run now but will be back in Salmon come June. We can catch up then. Bye."

Chapter Sixty-Four

Soya and the boys boarded their secure flight to the USA. As soon as they reached altitude, Soya's FBI escorts brought her to an area on the plane where there was a desk so they could deal with another thick file of papers to be signed, passports for each of them, and the most important thing to Soya—the location of their new home.

"Well, Mrs. Allem, I think the news I have for you is positive. You had requested employment in the area of finance in your new hometown. As you likely know, the best city in the United States to pursue this profession is New York. Because of your exceptional record at Stanford, we have managed to place you in an entry-level position with one of the world's largest investment banks. We were also fortunate to find a home for you near the rail line to the city but in a smaller town where we feel it would be more pleasant for your boys and much more reasonable to live than in Manhattan. It will also be more secure."

Her thoughts jumped from coast to coast. She had dreamed of a return to the San Francisco area, but she knew New York was the place to be if she was to start the career she had always planned on having before her unexpected "exodus" to Iran. It didn't take her more than a few seconds to decide she could, on occasion, make the six-hour cross-country flight to visit old friends and still have her career.

"Sounds great," she responded after a few moments of uncomfortable silence. "Just give me all the details you can, especially when they expect me to report to work. I'm sure you'll at least give me a few weeks to get settled and for my boys to acclimate a bit."

"No problem, Mrs. Allem...or should I say Mrs. Aspen? Yep, that's your new name."

The agent opened her passport, and she read her new name, Sharon Aspen, on her passport. Along with her new address, 1230 Oak Avenue, Fort Carson, New York. It really felt strange. After thirty-one years as Soya, it was suddenly Sharon. *Oh well*, she thought, *at least the initials are the same.*

The plane landed at a private airport in Westchester County. The four of them were taken from the plane to a waiting SUV, where airport personnel loaded their luggage in the rear. Within minutes, the agents drove them off to their new home. Soya found herself alone with her thoughts while the boys gazed in amazement at their new country and thought how different it was from the old buildings in central Paris where they had been living for the past few months.

Chapter Sixty-Five

Jamie and Emma had just finished their tour of France and were back at Orly to board their flight to the States. They would spend a day in New York to catch a Broadway musical before completing the trip to Idaho. The past two weeks had been a blast, but Emma was ready for home, as she dreamed of Mo every day. It seemed that no matter how the good times rolled with Jamie, she simply couldn't get past the romantic feelings she had for Mo.

They landed at JFK and cabbed into town. Jamie had made reservations at the Plaza in a junior suite overlooking Central Park. They played out the New York scene with everything from pastrami on rye at Katz's Deli to beautiful duckling at the Four Seasons. By the time they left town, they had each added a couple of pounds to the waistlines they had already expanded in the French countryside.

Their plane soared into the sky from LaGuardia heading to Boise. The Duncans picked them up at the airport there and whisked them home with nonstop chatter about every detail in their lives, from their time in Paris to their whirlwind time in New York City. As they entered Salmon, Emma began to get those same warm feelings she had had on her last trip back. When they passed Mo's shop, she stared intently, hoping he would step outside, but it wasn't to be. *Soon*, she thought, *I'll find a way for us to hold each other.*

Three days into their stay in Salmon, Jamie received an emergency phone call from Langley. He was ordered to report immediately to the New York office regarding a case he had been working on for months. Apparently, it was coming to a head, and his presence was required. It meant he would be missing four days in Salmon. Emma feigned a cry as he flew off, knowing this would be her chance to see Mo. As it turned out, Mo joined Emma in taking Jamie to the airport just as they had done as he left for Saudi before. As soon as Jamie's plane was in the air, the illicit lovers were in the car, holding each other with a passion that had been held in check for so long it simply exploded.

They hugged and kissed and wept with joy at their moment of release. If ever there had been happiness in their lives, it peaked at that moment.

Chapter Sixty-Six

Emma called home to excuse herself from spending time with the family, saying that she, Mo, and their friends had a lot of catching up to do. In reality, of course, the catching up was only with Mo, and it was in a straight line that they traveled from the airport to their personal hideaway in the tiny town of Cobalt, just south of Salmon. Now they would have the entire afternoon and evening to make love and make plans for the future.

*****

While they were attending to their lives, Jamie was landing a few hours later at the same military airport not far from Manhattan that had welcomed Soya when she arrived from Paris. He was soon in his room at the Sofitel Hotel in Downtown Manhattan, where he would meet the team he had been leading for months. The conspirators in this case were being led to the same hotel by an agent posing as a banker who would be laundering money for their terror cell based in Paris. Jamie's crew would be taping them in an adjoining room as they finalized the deal they thought they were making with a major bank that was known for some shady practices, especially in its home base of Switzerland, where hiding money from all sorts of folks was a major business.

The men involved had a quick dinner in the hotel restaurant then came upstairs to conclude the deal. As they finished their nefarious business and shook hands, Jamie and his crew burst through both the front and adjoining doors to the room, expecting no resistance. In seconds, a major terrorist money source was expected to be cut off. As they sprung through the doors, the terrorists produced weapons and fired at the CIA attackers. This "sure thing" suddenly became a live-fire engagement. Jamie pulled his service pistol and fired point-blank at the closest target, hitting him square between the eyes. As he did, he saw Jim Allen, one of his team, grab his chest and fall forward, smashing the coffee table in front of him. Another of his team caught a shot in the shoulder before the second terrorist was down and the fight ended. At the same time, the Paris police, joined by Interpol, raided the group's hideout in the Marais district of Paris, nabbing a dozen men who would soon be spending the rest of their lives in prison.

When the excitement ended, and Jamie was finally alone, he decided he sorely needed a cocktail or two. With fond memories of the beautiful bar at the Four Seasons restaurant, he grabbed a cab and soon was at the bar ordering a double gin gimlet straight up. After downing two of the potent drinks, he walked over to the restaurant side of the room and was seated at a small table that faced the entrance. He scanned the menu, placed his order, and looked up to see a familiar face staring back at him. It was Soya (he did not yet know her new name), first with a look of surprise and then with a huge smile on her face. She, along with her team at the bank, had just finished a retirement dinner, and the group was heading home. She excused herself and quickly made her way to Jamie's table. He rose, smiled, and gave her a hug that lasted a bit longer than it probably should have.

"Please join me," he said. "I can't believe you're hiding here in plain sight. You'll have to excuse my appearance, but I've had quite a night and have been drowning my sorrows at the bar. We can talk while I eat and try to catch up later."

"I would love to," said Soya, "but I'll have to check with Joan, my babysitter, to see if she can stay late."

An hour later, Jamie and Soya entered his room. They sat on the couch, and Jamie's first words were, "Who are you now?"

She smiled and said, "New words, same monogram... Sharon Aspen. The boys are now Sam, Henry, and Johnny. So even though our complexions may belie the words, we are indeed an all-American family."

"Hey, I think that's great," said Jamie. "But tell me, how are those boys adjusting to so many changes? After all, in less than a year, they've been residents of three very different countries."

"To be honest, Jamie, it hasn't been that easy for them. The fact that there are three of them does help, but getting their English up to speed and making new friends once again has been tough. That's especially true for Abdullah. The younger boys will start school and make friends more naturally. Abdullah—sorry, Sam—is falling in with kids who have already started the bonding process. It will surely take him a bit longer."

Soya went on to tell Jamie about where they were living and gave him their address and her phone numbers—both at home and work. Before they realized it, three hours had passed, and it was midnight.

Jamie asked, "Hey, does your babysitter expect you home by a certain time? I really didn't realize how long we had been talking."

"Oh my," she replied, "she expected me back two hours ago. May I use your phone?"

"Of course," Jamie replied.

After an apology and a brief discussion, Soya arranged for Joan to spend the night and pledged to pay her a bonus for this arrangement. The sitter would see the boys off to school, and Soya would take a personal day the next day to go home, change, and be ready for the office the following day.

"Jamie," she asked, "do you think I can get a room here at this late hour?"

"Maybe," he replied, "but I heard there are several conventions in town, so it could be tough. Let me call and see if I can twist some arms."

The call was met with a very decided no! Jamie told Soya, "I was just informed that the nearest available hotel room to Manhattan is some twenty miles away. I even tried to bribe him with an overpayment, but it didn't work. Look, there are two double beds in this room. You are certainly welcome to share. I'll even provide the toothpaste. No one has to know. Are you okay with that?"

"I guess I don't have much choice," she said, as she tried to conceal a smile that was forcing its way out. "Which bed is yours?"

"I'll take the one by the window," Jamie said.

Chapter Sixty-Seven

It was 10:00 p.m., and Emma found herself warm and happy in Mo's arms as he spooned her in their special place. When she saw the time, she nearly jumped out of bed.

"Mo," she said, "it's 10:00 and we have an hour's ride to get home. I hate to leave this bed, but we can't become suspect."

"I know," he said grudgingly, "but it's hard to leave heaven, don't you think?"

"It is, honey," she replied, "but if we don't do it, heaven could become hell. We're too close to allow that to happen, and I think our plan will work well. We just need a little more time to make it happen."

"Okay, I'm coming, but I must say I don't like the idea of moving from this wonderful warm spot."

"I know," said Emma as she came up behind him and kissed his cheek. Then she started to tickle her very ticklish lover, forcing him to jump out of bed with a huge smile on his face as he laughed uncontrollably.

Mo's car came quietly into town at 11:15 p.m. He dropped Emma at her parents' house and reluctantly moved on to his house, where he would spend the night dreaming of the hours he had just passed.

*****

At the same time, Jamie rose to use the bathroom. There was just enough light in the room that allowed him to see his beautiful roommate asleep in the bed next to his. As he returned to bed, he heard her say, "I really haven't been able to sleep very well. I think I must be on a guilt trip for losing track of time and all."

"Me too," said Jamie. "Not for that reason but because of all the excitement of the day followed by our unexpected meeting at the restaurant and all your exciting news."

As he talked, he unconsciously walked over and sat on the edge of her bed. All he was wearing were pajama bottoms. Soya had been in the habit of sleeping naked for as long as she could remember. While Jamie had been cleaning up for bed, she had gone under the covers this way without much thought. He was unaware.

As Jamie's eyes became accustomed to the dark, he could see that she was now wide awake. She had also moved a bit in bed, and in doing so, one breast had become exposed. Jamie wasn't sure if he should say something or do something. His rapidly forming erection suggested the latter.

The talking stopped. He looked into her eyes and leaned down to kiss her. She didn't withdraw. He then cradled her beautiful face in his hands and kissed her again. This time, she responded. As his hand found her breast, their breathing became heavy. Jamie pulled back the sheets and lay beside her. She reached for him and found him hard and ready. She relieved him of his pajama bottoms, and then the ritual began in earnest. Touching, kissing, holding on for fifteen minutes of incredibly sensual foreplay before penetration. The ecstasy that followed was well beyond what either of them had ever experienced. When it was over, they laid together truly breathless and wet with joy.

Finding the right words at this moment seemed impossible.

Chapter Sixty-Eight

It was 8:00 a.m. and Jamie had showered and dressed for a meeting at the CIA offices in New York. When he clicked his briefcase closed, Soya stirred from a deep sleep, looked at him, and smiled.

"I guess we were bad last night," she said in a throaty early morning voice. "I must admit feeling guilty for our pleasure. How about you?"

Jamie thought a moment and finally said, "I guess I do, but to be honest, not completely. The truth is that ever since Emma lost the baby, things have never really been the same between us. What you've seen on the surface does not reflect what's really been going on. The problem, of course, is how or if we will be able to carry on this special relationship. The first question I would have for you is whether you want to be with me. If you do, it will require a good deal of thought and planning."

Soya didn't say a word. She arose from bed and approached Jamie. He stared at her, captivated by her incredible beauty. She pressed her naked body against him, kissed him longingly, and wrapped her arms firmly around his neck. "Does that answer your question?" she whispered.

"I'll be in touch very soon," he replied.

Chapter Sixty-Nine

It took Jamie the final week of his R&R time to clean up the details of his now completed mission and pay a visit to the wife of his deceased CIA partner.

The revised plan was for Jamie and Emma to fly separately to Paris and meet up at their apartment. Jamie would have to go right back to work while Emma had another month to plan her next semester at the American school. She decided she also would spend that month taking a special condensed course on creating French pastries at the Le Cordon Bleu.

Jamie, on the other hand, was about to experience another career surprise. As he entered his office, he found Stu sitting in his chair.

"Uh-oh," he said, "the last time I walked in on you like this, I found myself moving from Tehran to Paris. That was great news. What's this about?"

"Well, my boy," started Stu, "I hope you won't be upset with this one. I'm afraid you and I will be working on a special project together."

"Hey, that'll be great," replied Jamie. "When and where?"

"When starts now for planning purposes. Where is back in the States...New York City, in particular. It's an important project, Jamie, and may well take a year or two to complete. Are you up for a little home cooking?"

"Well, I love the cooking here, but I must admit that making a home in New York is something I've dreamed about ever since college. I'm all in, but what about Emma?"

"I knew you'd ask, so I can tell you we've arranged a job at a high-end private school in Manhattan where we will both be stationed. Let me also tell you that I'm glad we'll be living on the government's dime. The price of apartments in the city is just off the charts. But with the kind of money the government should recoup when we eventually break this case, the rent will seem like small change."

After Stu left, Jamie immediately thought of how to break the idea of moving to New York to Emma. At least he wouldn't have to take the blame for the location as it wasn't his call. Then his thought quickly switched to Soya. *How extraordinary*, he thought. All he had to do was to figure out whether he should carry on an affair or divorce Emma and start a new life in the city where he had always wanted to be. Now he had the opportunity to do so with a woman who would be the perfect partner—smart, beautiful, with a built-in family, and who also shared the same career path he had always planned on at Stanford. And yes, they even shared the same college degree. Could it be more perfect?

Then his mind switched back to Emma—also beautiful and smart and, until now, the love of his life. But truth be told, some bad history had taken its toll on them. The likelihood of that history being erased, he knew, was a pipe dream. He also knew that even though Emma might accept the idea of living in New York, she would never really be happy there. The crazy buzz of that city was okay for her if it was just a few days as a tourist. A full-time situation would soon become a chore for her.

As he thought it through, he decided to call Soya. He picked up his office phone with a secure line and called her at work.

"Sharon Aspen," she answered.

"Jamie Duncan," he responded.

"Oh my, I didn't expect to hear from you so soon. How are you?"

"At this moment, flying high. I can't talk long but wanted you to know that I'll be coming to New York City soon on a semipermanent basis. I'll fill you in later. Love you. Bye."

Soya heard the *click* and sat there staring at her phone. *What just happened?* she wondered to herself. And was it as wonderful as it seemed?

Chapter Seventy

Jamie came home that night at the usual time. Emma came in a few minutes later holding a small box.

"Hi, honey," she said, offering a small peck on the cheek. "Would you like to see the first of the many pastry delights your wife will be producing?"

Her happy mood was infectious, and Jamie—always interested in fine food—responded, "Feed me, feed me."

She opened the box and presented four perfectly frosted petits fours in four different flavors.

"They started with the easy ones," she offered, "which also happen to be among our favorites. I saw some things that the advanced classes had done. I'm not sure that I'll ever be that accomplished."

"No need, Em," said Jamie as he wolfed down a chocolate version with white buttercream frosting. He then pushed the box away, knowing he could finish all of them if they were in arm's reach.

"You'd better put something healthy on the table," he pleaded, "before I get myself in trouble."

"I thought we'd just go out," replied Emma. "I think I've had too much kitchen time for today. Why don't we go back to that bistro we went to the first day I came to Paris?"

"Okay, kid. It's a date. Let me change, wash up, and we'll be off."

As Jamie stood in the bathroom, looking at himself in the mirror, he began to have a strange feeling. With all his other indiscretions, they were just spur-of-the-moment situations without any serious feelings involved. He never really felt like he was cheating. It was all just a means of satisfying a basic human need. Now it was different—very different! Soya had truly taken Emma's place in his heart and mind. As he looked at himself, he found he was searching for a way to justify what he was doing. He wondered if he could live with himself if he was the villain in his mind. He knew he had to somehow lay the blame on Emma so he could free himself to live a happy life. It was a new kind of self-imposed torture. Now he had to go merrily down the street with Emma while all he wanted was to be with Soya.

He washed with warm water then splashed cold water on his face to shake himself out of this thought pattern. He threw on jeans and a T-shirt, then announced that he was ready for dinner. The walk proved to be quiet. They held hands all the way while dreaming of their respective brown-skinned lovers. The irony was something to behold, yet neither of them suspected that it existed.

As they started in on dessert, Jamie decided to break the news about New York to Emma. He knew her initial reaction would be negative but wanted to see if she, after thinking it through, would accept the idea or want to call it quits. If it was the latter, he would pretend to be hurt but would acquiesce and agree to a divorce. If, however, she agreed to the move, he would have much more to consider.

Oh well, he thought to himself, *we shall soon find out. Here goes!*

"Em," he started, "something happened at work today…something big. I don't know much yet in the way of details, but I can tell you that it will require us to move again." With this, he paused and looked into her eyes. She didn't move. The ice cream and the spoon that held it stopped in midair.

A moment of nonresponse ended with a single word, "Where?"

"New York City."

The spoon stayed in space. Only her jaw dropped. Finally, she said, "Jamie Duncan, did you request New York?"

"I knew you would ask that," he responded, "but the answer is a definite no. When I walked into my office, I found Stu, my old boss from Tehran, sitting in my chair. He gave me the news pretty much the way he did before. He even has a job for you in one of those uppity private schools in Manhattan. Look, I know you've never been a big fan of New York, but look at how you've done in Paris. I know it's prettier here than in New York, but it's still big-city living. And as you know by now, I have no choice in my assignment locales. Anyway, I wanted to give you as much time as possible to think about it. Stu said he and I would have to head back home next week to prepare the project. It will probably take two to three weeks of prep time. Then I'll be back here for a couple of weeks to take care of our personal business and get ready to move. Please, please give it some thought without us getting into an argument. As soon as

I know more details, I'll get you up to speed so that when I come back, we can discuss everything in a sensible way."

Emma remained mute. As the ice cream began to drip on the table, she caught herself and put the spoon down.

"I'm going to the ladies' room," she said quietly. "When I come back, we should go home."

The evening ended in indecisive silence.

Chapter Seventy-One

The next week passed quietly. Emma didn't ask, and Jamie offered nothing new. When he left the house on his way from Paris to the military airport in New York City, they hugged with little emotion, and Jamie promised more details after he was in the States and given further briefings on the project.

Once the door was closed between them, all Jamie's thoughts transferred to Soya, and all of Emma's to Mohammed.

The CIA owned the plane Jamie was on. It allowed Stu and Jamie to start reviewing the purpose, scope, and players in the project. With Iran at the heart of the problem, it soon became apparent to Jamie why he and Stu were selected to direct the project.

At the same time that this new project was getting started, it turned out that the US government had decided to go along with the prisoner exchange for Ken Griffin. Five Iranian spies had been held in US jails for a number of years. Iran offered Griffin in exchange for these men. Soon after working out the agreement, all parties met at a neutral desert site on the Saudi-Iran border. There was a discussion between the parties during the exchange that lasted for approximately ten minutes. Each party then loaded their people onto their respective SUVs and left the meeting place. Five minutes later, the SUV with Ken Griffin aboard exploded. It turned out that while the discussion between the parties took place, Iranian commandos had placed four land mines on the exit road. Ken Griffin and the three Navy SEALs who accompanied him were killed instantly. Now, both as a matter of revenge and in an effort to quash a money-laundering scheme that Iran had been conducting in both the United States and Canada, the CIA was going to come down hard by cutting off a source of much-needed funds the Iranian government had been collecting.

The plan was elaborate, involving many CIA people along with the Royal Mounted Police. Stu's apartment in Manhattan was large and was not only to be his home but headquarters for the operation. His bedroom and bathroom were private areas with the rest of the five-bedroom apartment to be set up as an office. It was in the process of being specially wired for all the equipment needed to spy on the Iranians whose office for the laundering operation was in the same building. Jamie's apartment was just a block away and was a modest though a comfortable two-bedroom unit. Emma's school, should she agree to come, was within walking distance of their apartment.

It would likely be close to a month before all furniture and personnel would be in place, so Stu and Jamie were set up in a nearby hotel, allowing them to finalize all the plans, meet all the personnel to be involved, and review the background material on the money-laundering scheme.

Obviously, Jamie could only pass along information to Emma about their apartment and the school. Years before, he would have put everything into this effort. Today, however, he was really hoping she would turn him down and agree to a divorce. Only his intense sense of guilt had him continue the charade.

Before he called Emma, however, he wanted to see Soya again to be sure everything in their relationship was still on track.

They agreed to meet at her home. Jamie wanted to see the boys again and then share with her the idea that he would likely be involved with a top-secret project in New York City for an extended period of time. He explained that he did not yet know if Emma would agree to come along as she had never wanted to live in the city. In either case, he said, he wanted to be with Soya forever and hoped that a divorce from Emma could be worked out quickly. If not, he would want to see her anyway until he could figure a way out of his marriage.

They sat in a quiet corner of a nearby suburban restaurant as Jamie laid out the situation as best he could. The two of them kept looking at each other, holding hands, not wanting to be apart for even a moment, knowing they had finally found in each other the perfect partnership.

As they parted that evening, they planned a weekend together in New England.

Jamie knew Stu would be going back to Paris for some meetings and that he would not be needed on those particular dates. He surely didn't want Stu to be aware of his infidelity, or especially that it was with an Iranian in hiding because of her familial ties to their previous Iranian assignment. If Stu caught even the smallest sense of Jamie's affair, it would bring unwanted suspicion on him.

Chapter Seventy-Two

Three weeks passed. The special weekend came and went and left Jamie and Soya closer than ever before. It also brought the time of reckoning with Emma to a head. Jamie had advised her that he would arrive on a Saturday and that they should plan on talking through the situation over the weekend so he could make final arrangements for moving.

The CIA driver picked him up at the private airport and brought him home just after 10:00 a.m. on Saturday. His mind was spinning with all the possibilities that this weekend could bring.

The old elevator stopped, and he opened the gate. Emma must have heard it as she had opened the door and stood, waiting for him in the doorway.

"Hi, Em," he said as he approached her, kissed her on the cheek, and continued into the apartment.

Emma caught up with him in the bedroom as he began to unpack his suitcase. "How are things in the big city?" she asked.

"Oh, pretty much as expected. Lots of work and even more pressure to get it done as quickly as possible. Best part has been working with Stu again. You have to be lucky to have a boss who can be so professional and be a true friend at the same time. But right now, as important as this work is going to be, I am most concerned about us. I hope you've given the idea of being in New York for an extended period, probably a year or two, some serious thought. I can tell you that the apartment they have for us is very nice and just a block from where I'll be working and within easy walking distance to the school where you'd be teaching. I can also tell you that the school is considered the very best in the city. I had a meeting with the headmaster, who was a very likable fellow. After reviewing your résumé and recommendations from both Salmon and Paris, he said he was thoroughly impressed and looked forward to having you on his staff. All that said, however, the final word is with you, Em. I really must know your decision. It means everything to me and will dictate how our lives are going to move forward."

Emma looked him straight in the eye for a few moments without saying a word. She then began to slowly pace the room and give her response, "Jamie, so many things have been going through my mind these last few weeks, so many thoughts going back to the day we first met. So many good things and so many bad. And now that I've learned to enjoy Paris, you want me to follow you to another big city, one with neither the grace nor beauty of Paris. It's a city of shrill noises, harsh people, and a pace of life so different from what I love about my home town. The question keeps coming back to me. *Do I stay with the man I married, or do I go home to the place I love?* If the bad things in our history hadn't happened, the need to choose between these two things would not be an issue. I would always choose you. But these things have happened, and they just can't be erased. They must be seriously considered. I've been debating this situation ever since you left. So here's my decision. I'll give New York no more than one year. If things are good, I'll continue and hope that our marriage survives and thrives. If things do not work out, I'll ask you for a divorce, and we can restart our lives. What do you say to that?"

Jamie struggled to find the right thing to say. After a minute or so, he responded, "Em, that's the second time you've inserted the word *divorce* into one of our discussions. It's a very hurtful word for me. In the time we've had together in Paris, I thought that much of the hurt had faded away. Perhaps some of it has but obviously not as much as I had hoped. I'm glad you'll come back with me, and I promise to do everything within my power to bring us back to where we once were. If we can't get there, then I agree that restarting our lives separately would make the most sense. But let's really give it a try, okay?"

"I will, Jamie, I will," she replied. And with that response, she approached him, hugged him firmly, and held on until they both collapsed onto the bed. They made love with their bodies while their minds floated to others they loved more.

Chapter Seventy-Three

The last of the furniture and personal belongings had just left the apartment. Everything was to be flown to New York and be in place before they arrived. They each had one suitcase they would take to the Ritz Hotel for their last night in Paris. They had both always wanted to stay at the opulent Parisian landmark before they left, and this seemed to be their last chance. Jamie had arranged for a junior suite overlooking the Place Vendôme, where one could observe some of the most luxurious shops in Paris. In this place, window-shopping would be the most they could afford, but it was fun.

After an hour's stroll on the Avenue, they decided to return to the hotel and have a swim in the beautifully designed indoor pool. They found themselves the only swimmers that day and had an unusually playful time, pretending this was their home and that the pool was theirs alone. After a while, they returned to their room, showered, put on the plush hotel robes, and ordered room service. It was as nice a start to their renewed pledges to one another as there could be. It also felt incredibly strange.

Twenty-four hours later, they landed at JFK. A cab ride through rush-hour traffic was the first wake-up call for Emma as she began to shape her vision of life in Manhattan.

Jamie turned the keys to two locks as they entered their apartment. Jamie had given the movers the schematic of where the furniture should be placed. For the most part, they had followed instructions. The pile of boxes, however, presented a more daunting task. Even though the rooms where the boxes should have been placed were clearly indicated, all of them had been piled in the living room. Another welcoming note, thought Emma, from the crass psyche of New York City.

Too tired to deal with the mess after so long a day, they decided to stop in at EAT—a great deli/restaurant—for a sandwich and a piece of homemade apple pie. It wasn't the Ritz, but it sure did go down easy.

Chapter Seventy-Four

Before leaving for work, Jamie moved the boxes to their appropriate rooms, wolfed down some coffee, kissed Emma good-bye, and wished her luck with the hours of unpacking to come. On the way to work, he stopped at a pay phone in a nearby hotel and called Soya. Like most in the financial industry, she was in her office before the market opened.

"Sharon Aspen," she answered.

"Jamie Duncan," he replied.

"Oh, you're back. I'm so glad. When can I see you? I have to find out how things went with You-Know-Who."

"I know," he replied. "I'll give you the whole story in person in about a week. I have to get a schedule together so I can determine a safe time. I'll call you as soon as possible. Just know that I miss you like crazy and can't wait to see you."

"Me too," she responded. "Love you."

They hung up.

*****

As Jamie left the hotel, Emma was descending in the building elevator. Their phone was going to be installed later that day, and she wanted to call Mo and update him on the situation. She stopped in at a small grocery store and talked them into a few dollars' worth of change. She then entered the same hotel Jamie had just left, found the same telephone booth, and called Mo at home. She hadn't considered the time differences between New York and Salmon, so when he answered, Mo had just stepped out of the shower and was soaking wet.

"Hello," he barked, wondering who would be calling him at home at so early an hour.

"It's me, my love. I'm in New York and have so much to tell you, but I'm on a pay phone. Will you call me tomorrow after 10:00 a.m. our time, and I'll tell you everything. Our number is going to be [212] 555-3377 and will be installed this afternoon. Jamie should be at work first thing tomorrow morning, but in case he answers, just hang up."

"I love you, honey. I'll call you at 10:00 a.m. on the dot."

On the way home, Emma stopped by the same small grocery store. She picked up some of the basics and trudged home to begin the daunting job of setting up her new home.

The phone people showed up at 1:00 p.m. and were done by 2:00 p.m. Emma then called the headmaster at school to set up an appointment for the following afternoon. By dinnertime, she had lined shelves and drawers and had emptied half the boxes.

*****

When Jamie returned from a tiring day, they agreed to grab a cab and head over to a food emporium called

Zabar's. Jamie had heard about it at the office. The place was extraordinary. It had a buzz about it that reflected the action of the city. There were glorious and massive displays of foods the two of them had never seen before, all at amazingly high prices. By the time they left, they had spent more than $200. When they came back to the apartment, they were starving. The food didn't disappoint. They now had a special go-to place for whenever they were feeling flush.

Jamie mustered up enough energy to connect the TV sets and radios before flopping on the couch to watch some sitcoms and the local news. The next day would be an important day for both of them, especially Emma.

Chapter Seventy-Five

Emma sat next to the phone, anxiously awaiting Mo's call. As promised, the ring came as the clock struck 10:00 a.m.

"Hello," she answered.

"It's me, honey," Mo replied.

"Right on time, Mo. Thanks."

"Tell me what's happening and how your situation is playing out."

"Well, I think we're on our way to success. I told Jamie that I would try it for no more than a year…which means it could also be less. We have a decent apartment in a location that's convenient to the school where I'll be teaching and just a block from Jamie's office. From all appearances, everything would seem to be fine, except for one critical issue."

"And what might that be, my love?"

"It's you, Mo. It's not you that I'm living with. This whole thing is so crazy. But now we can at least have a legitimate way out. I told Jamie in no uncertain terms that if living in New York doesn't work out, we should get a divorce and start over. And he agreed. That still leaves the issue of our parents and all those relationships, but I think we just have to face that music. What I see is cutting things off here in the next six months, my moving back to

Salmon, and you and I getting married a year later, after everything else settles down and there's no trace of our past relationship."

"Sounds like a plan, Em. I hope I can wait without exploding with desire for you. I love you so much."

"Me too, Mo. Me too. But till then, I'll keep you up to date as much as possible. Now I have to get ready for a meeting with the headmaster of my new school. Hopefully, I'll get a nice group of kids to deal with. It will help to offset the pain of dealing with this crazy city. Goodbye, honey."

"Bye, Em. Miss you already."

The meeting at school went well. The headmaster was very pleasant. He took Emma on a tour of the school, which was truly ahead of its time with regard to equipment and all sorts of modem technology. Emma was able to observe the kindergarten class, where most of her students were currently enrolled. Their learning curve was such that these younger students were doing work that the first- and some second-grade students in Salmon were just being exposed to. She thought, *What a treat it will be to work with such smart children.*

*****

While Emma was at school, Jamie was buried in paperwork as the details of his new assignment began to take shape. He and Stu worked well together and found themselves running ahead of schedule. A few more days would see a finished plan that they would submit to Langley. As part of this, there was a recommendation for personnel that they thought would be best for the program. Once the plan and people were approved, it would be a matter of interviewing everyone that would be involved to be sure the right choices had been made. The toughest part would be to find two men who were fluent in Farsi. They had one agent they knew pretty well and had confidence in his ability. The second fellow was one of the Iranian contacts Jamie had worked with when he first went to Iran. Ensuring his loyalty was the biggest issue. If he turned out to be a weak link, all could be lost. His name was Ashraf Abbas, Jamie's first driver to Tehran.

Chapter Seventy-Six

One week later, Stu and Jamie were ready to present their plan to Langley. Most important for Jamie, he had a sense of what the short-term work schedule would be. One week from then, Stu would ostensibly be spending three days in the Saudi embassy interviewing Abbas. It would be during the week, so Emma would be at school, and he could steal away to see Soya under the guise of doing business. After that, he didn't know when he would be sure of any free time. He called Soya from his favorite pay phone in the hotel, and they set a time to meet.

Langley requested just a few minor changes to Jamie and Stu's plan, and it received a stamp of approval the day after the presentation. Jamie was able to start interviews in the States while Stu prepared for his trip to Riyadh. Things went along smoothly, and finally, the time to spend with Soya arrived. Jamie kissed Emma goodbye in the morning, saying he had more interviews to conduct out of town and would return in three days but would call her each day.

He packed his bag and with great anticipation, drove to see Soya, who had arranged to take three vacation days. She had also arranged for her sitter to stay with the boys. When the boys were settled with Joanie, a sitter they had quickly grown to love, Soya called a cab for a quick ride to a local McDonald's. Jamie was parked there, anxiously awaiting her arrival. After an hour's ride, they found themselves at Canoe Bay, a remote, rustic inn known for both its fine food and privacy for its guests.

They checked in, dropped their suitcases, and just stood inside the doorway of their cottage, holding each other firmly, not wanting to let go. These few days, they knew, were going to be very special, and they didn't want to waste a second.

Chapter Seventy-Seven

Jamie didn't keep track of how many times they made love; he only knew that no matter how many times, it wasn't often enough. The bond that had been strong going into this brief tryst was now even more firmly cemented. Driving Soya back to a cabstand not far from her home was painful. As he watched her disappear into the cab and drive away, Jamie felt like he wanted to cry.

Chapter Seventy-Eight

It actually took Stu a week to feel comfortable enough to bring Ashraf Abbas, Jamie's former driver, back to the States. It took a special agreement to bring his wife and son along and to make them US citizens before he would budge.

In the meantime, Jamie combed through the details of the plan along with the history of the money-laundering activities that had been put together by the government. As he read through all the minutia, he was suddenly jolted upright. There were those letters again—IGO. And there was that name again—Ali Hassan, a friend of Mohammed's father. As it turned out, the CIA had never stopped tapping his phone. This isolated contact, as it turned out, was the touchstone that set the current operation Jamie and Stu were planning into motion. After a couple of years of tapping his calls, the CIA saw a pattern forming. (It also matched up with similar situations they had been tracking in other parts of the world.) Significant donations from IGO came to a Canadian bank on a regular basis. Two or three times a year, much smaller donations came to organizations associated with the US military. The US donations were legitimate. The money sent to Canada appeared to stop there until one day, an unrelated trace that had been set up in Iran picked up a wire transfer sent, in error, to an Iranian bank instead of directly to the Iranian treasury. It turned out to be a simple human error by a bank clerk that tied the Canadian bank to what was, in fact, its main office in Tehran. The amount transferred was identical—to the penny—to an amount wired the previous day from an IGO office in Salmon, Idaho, to Canada. Once these details were put together, surveillance in Salmon was increased significantly.

After reading and rereading this information, Jamie felt more than ever that Mo just had to know something about these guys. However, the fact that he had already denied any knowledge of them to Jamie made it impossible for him to pursue the issue with him. Chances were, he thought, if he was involved—even peripherally—he would let his compatriots know about the investigation and blow the operation. Jamie would have to find another way.

As he thought his way through the dilemma, Jamie hit upon an idea. To make it work, it would require a trip back to Salmon. He knew Emma would always be ready for a trip home, so he decided to use her as part of his plan.

Chapter Seventy-Nine

As Jamie began his plan for Salmon, Stu rushed into his office.

"Jamie," he said, "come here right now. We've got an old friend of yours paying us a visit."

Jamie ran into the next room where a monitor showed one of their new Iranian agents acting as a moneyman meeting with none other than Ali Hassan from Salmon, Idaho. Jamie didn't recognize the voice immediately, but when Hassan turned and faced the hidden camera, it all came into focus.

While the conversation was largely in Farsi, Jamie knew the language well enough that he could capture the meaning. The gist of it was that his man (Ashraf) was presenting himself as an official representative of the Iranian government and was aware of IGO's dealings with the Iranian branch in Canada (this bank had always presented itself as "independent" without any association to another bank in Canada or anywhere else in the world). He approached Hassan, he said, because they had discovered the considerable loss of funds to the government because the current bank took 30 percent of all IGO's contributions as fees for performing their money-laundering services. In contrast, he said he would act as an independent "money manager" on behalf of the Iranian government and would take only 5 percent as a handling fee. He too would be based in Canada but would have very little overhead and would be the official representative of the Iranian government. To verify his legitimacy, he presented to Ali Hassan several (forged) documents from the government signed by Khomeini himself.

After an extended conversation about how the operation would work with the original bank out of the picture, Hassan rose, said he would discuss this proposition with the other members of his IGO staff, and get back to him within a week's time. Also, without stating a name, Hassan said that if Ashraf needed to reach him and he proved unavailable, they could contact the son of his good friend in Salmon, whom they could trust with any information. He gave them a phone number that Jamie quickly jotted down.

Jamie knew who the friend's son was likely to be and dreaded the thought of one day arresting his oldest and closest childhood friend. He immediately checked his address book to compare the number with Mo's current number at home. They matched.

Chapter Eighty

The following Friday, Jamie and Emma boarded a commercial flight to Boise. They arrived at 7:30 in the evening and picked up a rental car. It was supposed to be a surprise visit for the parents, but in truth, it was a work visit for Jamie. Emma was just thrilled with the idea and with the fact that Jamie had finally done something he knew she would enjoy. In light of the positives, she didn't question the motivation. What she mostly cared about was a chance to spend some time with Mo.

When they arrived in Salmon, the first stop was at Jamie's parents' home. He thought they would fall over with joy when they opened the door to see Jamie and Emma looking back at them.

"What are you doing here?" they exclaimed.

"Oh, just a spur-of-the-moment decision," Jamie responded. "You know that sometimes home just keeps calling us back."

"How long can you stay?" asked Jamie's mom.

"We have a return flight on Sunday evening at 5:00. Unfortunately, we are still working for a living," Jamie said.

With that, they dropped their suitcases in the guest room while Jamie's mom called the Steeles to come right over.

As always, the evening with the six of them was fun-filled, with much happiness all around. At midnight, they called it quits. Saturday was to be busy, as Jamie and Emma planned to catch up with all their old friends.

They rose early the next morning, had a quick breakfast with the Duncans, and headed to town. The first stop, they agreed, was to visit Mohammed. Emma was both thrilled and somewhat terrified at the same time at the prospect of her two men being in the same room with her. At 8:00 a.m., they entered his shop. Mo was alone in back, so they rang the bell on the counter then hid like a couple of kids until he came up front.

With no one in view, Mo called out, "Can I help you?"

From his position in hiding, Jamie called back, "Probably not...I can only talk with the owner of this joint."

Mohammed knew the voice immediately. This was one of Jamie's old stunts when they were in high school.

"Okay, Duncan," he said, "come out with your hands up."

"Man, Mo, don't you ever forget a voice?"

The two of them shook hands and embraced.

Then from another secluded corner came Emma's voice, "Hey, don't I get to say hi too?"

Mohammed had to stop himself from jumping over the counter and sweeping her off her feet. Instead, he responded, "Ah, it sounds like a powerful woman, one strong as Steele."

Emma, a bit less able to contain her emotion, ran over and gave Mo the biggest hug.

"I'm so glad to see you, Mo. Seems like forever since we've been together."

"Sure does," he casually replied.

Jamie said, "Oh, I almost forgot that I have to call my office. You two talk. Mo, can I use your phone for just a minute?"

"Sure, Jamie. Why don't you use the one in my back office?"

"Thanks, Mo. It'll be perfect. You guys go ahead and catch up."

Jamie went in back, picked up the receiver of the rotary phone, and faked a business call. He spoke loudly so Mo could tell he was in a conversation. He then hung up and dialed another number. After a brief discussion, he returned.

"Em," he said, "I called home and made plans to have dinner with the folks tonight, but Dad also asked me to help with a repair he's doing at the house. It shouldn't take too long. Why don't you hang out with Mo, and I'll meet you back here as soon as we're finished?"

"Sounds perfect," she replied. And indeed it was for her and Mo.

Emma realized this was likely her only chance to be alone with her lover. Jamie, on the other hand, was really going to try to do some work on his operation by attempting to create a "casual encounter" with one Ali Hassan.

Hassan's office was just three blocks from Mo's shop. Jamie walked directly there and peered through the window. As luck would have it, Hassan was walking toward the door of his ground-floor office, briefcase in hand. Jamie stepped back, and as the door opened, he moved quickly forward, intentionally bumping into Hassan.

"Oh, excuse me," Jamie said. "Ah, Mr. Hassan, it's been a long time. I'm Jamie Duncan. Do you remember me? Mohammed Amsur and I were best friends in high school."

"Of course, I remember," he said. "How are you doing, my boy?"

"I'm doing very well, thanks. Just moved to New York from Paris a short time ago. The CIA sure does make folks move around."

"Ah, yes, now I remember. Mohammed mentioned that you were asking him about something to do with Iran, and he came to ask me about it. I couldn't believe that after all we went through to come here and earn our citizenship that they would think we would betray our loyalty to the United States."

"Yes, I know you wouldn't, but I was told to ask the question just to clear the air. Apparently, they had picked up something suspicious, but nothing has come of it as far as I know. I'm sure there's nothing for you to be concerned about."

"Well, I appreciate your support, Jamie. You've known our community here most of your life, and I'm sure you'd vouch for us to your CIA people."

"Absolutely, sir. And I hope you didn't think I was trying to run you down a moment ago. I just didn't see you coming."

"No problem. But I must be on my way. I was already late for a meeting. Hope to see you again soon."

With that, Hassan moved off quickly to his appointment. Jamie just stood there for a moment smiling to himself. Now he had done exactly what he had come here to do—plant a seed of doubt about the Canadian bank in Hassan's mind. Little did this man know, he thought, just how much he would never want to see Jamie again.

Only fifteen minutes had passed, so Jamie wandered around town until he had been gone half an hour before returning for Emma. When he entered the shop, a slightly disheveled Mohammed was waiting on a customer. About the time the customer left, Emma came from the back room, adjusting her sweater and then putting on some lipstick. When she looked up, she saw Jamie staring right back at her.

"Oh," she exclaimed. "That was quick. What did he need you to do?"

"Oh, he was fixing the outboard motor and needed help lifting it back on the boat."

"No big deal. Did you two get up-to-date?"

"Oh, yes, but I'm sure there's more ground to cover. Why don't we stop to see everyone else while Mo gets his work done? We can come back around noon and have lunch together. His girl will be in for the afternoon, so he can spend a little time with us."

"Sounds great," said Jamie. *Also seems a little strange*, he thought, *that Emma would have to replace lipstick she had just put on at home, not to mention the somewhat disheveled appearance of both her and Mo. Probably nothing there, but you never know.*

Chapter Eighty-One

Jamie and Emma left to catch their flight in Boise. Within fifteen minutes of their departure, Ali Hassan was knocking on Mohammed's door.

"We must talk immediately," Ali whispered to Mo as his last customer of the day left the shop.

"You look frightened," Mo responded. "What has happened?"

"It's your friend, Jamie. He met me, actually ran into me as I left my office. It was a brief conversation, but one that deeply concerned me. He said they had overheard a suspicious call, and that it came from their investigation of a Canadian bank. You know that it had to be our IGO bank. I'll have to do more checking, but we may have to make a change. Interestingly, I was recently approached by a man from our homeland who said he could handle our business and save us from the 30 percent fee we now pay for laundering services. He said he is an official government representative and would perform the same service, also out of Canada, for just 5 percent, significantly increasing the funds that would flow through for their intended purpose."

"But Ali," said Mo, "how do you know if this man is who he says he is?"

"At our meeting, he presented written documentation signed by Khomeini. I've seen his signature many times on a variety of documents and know well the unusual paper they use on official government documents. I also know that this man spoke with a true Iranian speech pattern... no foreign accent at all. And frankly, I know of no other alternative for us. If the CIA is, in fact, acting on leads from the bank, we should nullify our relationship and move as quickly as possible. I have discussed this with your father, and he agrees. Hopefully, it won't upset him too much, though he seemed quite worried...more for you than for himself. If anything were to come of this and affect your life, I fear he would never forgive himself."

*****

The following day, the man who had approached Ali Hassan received a call from him. He arranged to meet him at the New York office Jamie and Stu had set up in the hotel. Jamie overheard the recording of the conversation in Farsi and could tell that a meeting was in the process of being arranged. When his old Iranian contact hung up, Jamie approached him and said, "What's the deal?"

"Day after tomorrow, we're meeting here again with Hassan and another man he says is a lifelong friend and his partner in the IGO project."

Lifelong friend, Jamie assumed, would likely mean Mo's father. *Better him than Mo*, he thought to himself. *This is going to be important and also very uncomfortable for me on a personal level. Oh well, here goes everything.*

Chapter Eighty-Two

Emma sat down at the hotel phone booth and dialed Mo's number at the shop. "Can you talk?" she asked.

"Yes," he said. "I'm back in my office with the door closed. What is it, my love?"

"Well, it's probably nothing, but I noticed a strange look on Jamie's face when he came back to meet us at the shop. I think he saw me straightening my clothing, and I know he was wondering why I was putting on lipstick so soon after I had put it on at home. He asked me why, but I sort of changed the subject. It seems that ever since he's been involved in the intelligence business, even back to his army days, he observes things more closely. At times, it even feels a little creepy. Anyway, I just wondered if you sensed any concern on his part?"

"I can't say that I did, but one thing I can say is that I would never have given up holding you for the few minutes we had together. The way I ache for you every day of my life is so intense that I would never pass up such an opportunity."

"I know how you feel, honey. I have those same feelings all the time. Anyway, I'm glad you weren't concerned about Jamie. That makes me feel better. Now I must run back to school. We have a meeting about a problem student. Love you, Mo. Bye."

"Bye, Em."

That evening, Emma looked carefully at Jamie as he was wolfing down one of her now-famous French creations. Everything seemed to be normal. There was no interrogation that might indicate suspicion. She felt better.

Chapter Eighty-Three

Obviously, the one man who had to stay out of sight was Jamie. But he could see what was going on through the hidden camera in the room next door. He and Stu were front and center as they heard the knock on the door. The two men from Salmon were quickly ushered in by the Iranian undercover agent. The offering of tea and some social conversation about the homeland ensued before they got down to business.

Without any acknowledgment of the potential danger Ali had been led to perceive relative to the bank, he quickly got to the point. "Ashraf," he started, "my dear friend Mr. Amsur and I, along with others familiar with our operation, have decided that your offer would be best for the homeland. It would be our desire to start passing all contributions through your Canadian operation except, of course, for the 25 percentage we reserve for the US military people to preserve the appearance of legitimacy. Please tell me when we can start transferring funds so we can sever our relationship with the bank. We plan to do this simply by advising them that we are ceasing to function as a charitable organization and will, therefore, not be in need of their services any longer."

"I must tell you, Ali, that this is decidedly good news. I will advise our government of your decision and immediately travel to Toronto to acquire a small office space where the funds will be processed. It shouldn't take more than a month or so to set up our operation, but I'll call you in the next few days to give you our estimate on the timing. Meanwhile, I want you to know that in anticipation of your positive answer, the government has authorized me to take you to a celebratory dinner in honor of our new business arrangement. I understand you are staying at the Ritz. We will pick you up at 7:00 this evening."

*****

The four men said their good-byes. Once in a taxi, Ali Hassan said to his friend, "I noticed you didn't speak a word during our meeting. How do you feel about all these changes?"

"My dear friend, I don't know what choice we really had. What's more, in my weakened state, I don't know that I'll be around to see the result. All I can say is that I don't want Mohammed to be a victim of our actions. He is such a good man."

"I know, my friend. I'll do whatever I can to keep him safe. And as for you, no more talking of not being here. I can't allow such thoughts."

Chapter Eighty-Four

To close the trap on IGO, the government plan was to allow a period of time to go by, so a pattern of their deceitful practices could be established. The feds weren't quite sure exactly how often transfers were being made. Jamie and Stu suspected that five to six months would likely have to pass before they could close in. In the interim, they would leave their office set up in place. They would also keep the meeting room available in case it was needed later in the process.

As things were coming together a bit faster than originally expected, they now thought that three to four months would be an adequate time period to have enough evidence to proceed with an arrest. On the one hand, Jamie was happy for what appeared to be a successful operation. He was happy as well that the end of the operation might also mean the end of his marriage and a new life with Soya. The downside, however, was the possibility of his oldest friend going to jail if he was found to be involved.

*****

Emma, of course, had no idea about Jamie's work activities or his affair with Soya. She did at times wonder where she and her boys had been sent when they came to the United States, but she had no expectation of finding out given the secrecy of these relocation projects. Her only real concern was when and how she and Mo would be together. Then came a break. Jamie informed her that he would be away for a week on business. He was, in fact, traveling to Canada with his Iranian cohorts to set up their office. This meant that Mo could come to New York and spend time with Emma to make final plans for their future.

Emma reserved a room for Mo at the hotel where she had been using the phone booth. He had made plans for a five-night stay. He had never been to the big city, and she knew few people there. Therefore, they could move around rather freely without concern of being found out. Their excitement was palpable, and when Mo's cab arrived at the hotel, Emma was there to greet him. They checked in, and as soon as the bellman left the room, they held each other, loving the warmth of their bodies melding together.

"Well, Mo," Emma finally said, "I think this is the beginning of the end and the beginning of the beginning. We'll start tonight with a trip to my favorite New York deli and a night together that I'll never want to end."

At dinner, they talked nonstop about the city and every tourist place Emma would take her man. From that, they moved to more important issues—divorce, engagement, and marriage.

*****

Mo didn't want to spoil the first night but knew it was time to let Emma know about IGO. It would be a delicate and difficult conversation. His greatest fear was that his all-American girl would be offended by what she might well consider to be antiAmerican activities as opposed to, as Mo saw it, a pro-Iranian venture.

When they returned to the room, Emma began to get into more specific points when Mo said, "Let's wait until tomorrow, honey. It's been a long and tiring day. I'd rather devote my remaining energy to loving you and leave the details for tomorrow. What do you say?"

"I say that's the best idea I've heard all day."

Chapter Eighty-Five

On Mo's third day in town, Emma wanted to expand his cultural background with a few Hours at the Frick Art Museum followed by a lunch at Lady M…a Patisserie with a light luncheon menu. As they entered the Frick, once the luxurious mansion of a coal baron, Emma pulled up short. She wasn't sure, but she saw a woman who looked exactly like Soya. As they entered the first gallery, she walked to her right and almost ran into her friend. The two of them stared at each other in amazement, not knowing quite what to do. Then they forced smiles and hugged as though nothing had ever changed between them. Except, of course, that *everything* had.

While this encounter was going on, Mo stood staring at this beautiful woman and wondered what on earth was going on. Finally, Emma regained her composure enough to introduce Mo to Soya, who had just whispered her new name to Emma.

"Mo," said Emma, "Sharon was a friend of Jamie's that he met while he was working in the Middle East. It's a long story, but she was able to come to the States and start a new life here."

"Oh, I see," said Mo, "and what country did you come from?"

Sharon hesitated, then said, "Iran."

"Oh, assalamu alaikum, my countryman. I was born there as well but left long ago for Canada. Now I live in Idaho."

"So you and Emma must have met there. Did you live near her in Salmon?"

"Oh yes, we were in high school together there. That's where I met Jamie as well. We've all been friends for years. I just came to New York on a business trip for a few days, and Emma has been good enough to spend a day with me to sightsee. I've never been here before."

"Well, it will surely take you much more than one day to see New York. It really is quite a place to both see and learn."

"You're certainly right about that. After today, I think I'll need a good night's sleep before I return to a much different pace in Salmon."

"Well, it's been nice seeing you both," Soya said. "Unfortunately, I was just leaving before we bumped into each other. I have to get home before my boys get there."

With a quick hug for Emma and a handshake for Mo, Soya departed without a suggestion that she and Emma get together and catch up. All she could think of was keeping a calm demeanor long enough to get away from the wife of her lover.

On the other side of the coin, Emma was scared that word of her being with Mo would somehow get back to Jamie, though as far as she knew he hadn't had contact with Soya since she came over with the FBI agents.

"Oh, Mo," she cried, as she clung to his jacket. "I can't believe that in this huge city, I had to bump into one of only a handful of people I know here. And I didn't even know she lived in New York."

"Well, I obviously knew a little of your relationship, but I did know that if Jamie was to somehow find out I was here, we should have a cover story. That's why I said I was here on business and that I was going home tomorrow. That way, you can tell Jamie I was here to buy some equipment for my cleaning operation and surprised you while in town. Then you volunteered to show me the town, so I stayed for an extra day."

"Oh, Mo, you're right as usual. That's what I'll do. I feel better already. So let me take you through this fabulous place, and then I'll take you home and make you one of my famous French dinners."

"Sounds great, my love, as long as I can have you for dessert."

"My dear Mo, that is my specialty!"

Somehow Mo never got around to discussing IGO. He just couldn't interrupt the happiness with such talk.

Chapter Eighty-Six

When Jamie returned from Canada, his first stop was at the hotel with his favorite phone booth. He hadn't spoken with Soya for weeks and longed to hear her voice. She picked up her office phone, and as soon as she heard his voice, she gasped.

"Jamie," she whispered, "I must tell you what happened."

"You sound distressed, honey. What gives?"

"I was at the Frick, and of all people, guess who I ran into? Your Emma and her Iranian friend."

"Iranian friend...was it a man?"

"It was. His name was Mohammed. Said he was in town on business and was going back to Salmon the next day. He said he knew you from high school. I assume you know who I'm talking about."

"I do, indeed. My oldest friend. He, Emma, and I always hung out together all through high school. Strange, though, that he would be in New York on business. He just runs a small chain of cleaning and laundry locations in Idaho."

"Well, I just spoke with them briefly...gave Emma my new first name, but nothing more, not even where I'm living or even my last name. It was just a few minutes of social chatter, and I left as quickly as I could. As you might imagine, the whole situation was very uncomfortable for me."

"I understand. It will be interesting to see if she brings it up. Obviously, I'll let it slide for now."

Four months passed. Much as expected, the change in financial arrangements for IGO went smoothly. Jamie and Stu studied the transactions as they accumulated, recording every detail of the operation. To accumulate even more evidence against Ali Hassan, they feigned a problem and asked him to come back to New York to provide "direction" on how to handle an unusual donation they didn't want to discuss over the phone. The incriminating discussion that resulted gave them absolute confidence that their case would stick. Now came the plan for arrest.

They knew that headquarters for IGO was, in fact, a small room hidden behind a bookcase in Ali's Salmon office. It reminded them exactly of the type of situation one would find in an old *Sherlock Holmes* movie. They even knew how to access the room as a result of a phone conversation they had picked up between Ali and an unnamed party that sounded to Jamie very much like his dear friend Mohammed. He had not yet implied to anyone at the CIA the possibility that Mo was involved, but he knew in his heart that he had to be in on the deal.

Then Jamie had a thought. Without mentioning it to Stu, he was able to get permission to tap another line in Salmon—Mo's home number. If he was going to be indicted as part of this program, he wanted to either be sure of his feelings or allay those worrisome thoughts altogether. Unfortunately, it didn't take long. On the third day the tap was active, Mo received a most disturbing call. It came from a public phone in New York City. The voice of the lady in New York was unmistakable.

"Hello."

"Hi, Mo darling, it's me. Just needed to hear your voice again. I know it hasn't been that long since you were here, and we held each other, but I miss you so every night. I know it's crazy, but when Jamie's here sleeping next to me, I lie there and pretend it's you. But then I can't reach out and touch you. It's so frustrating."

"I know, Em, but it won't be much longer. At least we seem to have gotten away with that chance meeting at the Frick museum. And I'll never forget the evening we had together when you made that incredible chicken cordon bleu. And the dessert…my, my, my, best I've ever had."

"Oh, Mo, it was the best. I can't wait until we have it again."

"Me either."

"Uh-oh, there's someone staring at me in the phone booth. I think he's anxious to make a call. Goodbye, my love. Talk to you soon."

Jamie sat, mouth agape, IGO pushed to the back of his mind. Now he knew for sure that his wife and best friend were having an affair. *How long has this been going on?* he wondered. The more he thought about it, the more he built up steam. As he felt he was about to explode with anger, he came to a sudden realization—he was every bit as guilty as Mo. *Talk about a quandary.*

I can't believe this, he thought, *yet it really has happened.* Then the more he thought about it, the more it made sense.

He was always gone while Mo was always home. Emma lost the baby, at least in part because of him, and Mo gave her a shoulder to cry on. He was in the Middle East for a year. Mo was taking her to dinner and out for coffee every week. And the more Jamie thought about it, he realized that Mo was, in effect, her surrogate husband.

But logic doesn't always hold when you find that your wife and best friend have both been disloyal. So soon the rationalizations began to evolve, and quickly he felt he would have to find a way to punish them for what they had done. And now he had the proof he needed to divorce Emma with cause while putting Mohammed in jail for his criminal activity with IGO.

Chapter Eighty-Seven

The case was coming together. Plans for the arrest of the small group that comprised the IGO staff were being formulated. Jamie, Stu, and several other CIA agents would be involved with the positioning of the group and timing for the arrest. As far as they could tell, none of the parties involved were armed, so while agents would have pistols, no one expected a shoot-out.

When all plans were completed, Jamie came home one evening and hinted that he was missing his parents and would like to go home for a few days. He knew Emma would jump at the chance, and as soon as the idea passed his lips, she was on the phone to their travel agent. The big day would come in two weeks.

Jamie assumed she would soon be on the phone to Mo to tell him the good news. He arrived at his office the next day at around 11:00 a.m. A light was flashing on his tape machine, meaning that a call had been picked up on Mo's line. Here's how it went:

"Hello."

"Mo, I'm coming home in two weeks!"

"What's happened?"

"Jamie said that even though he saw his folks only a few months ago that he somehow feels homesick and thinks it would be great if we could spend a few days with them. That means I can see you, my love, even if it won't be for long."

"Well, Em, maybe it should be for a long time. You said you would let him know if things weren't working out after six months. It's now been seven months. This could be just the right time to let them all know. What do you say?"

"Okay, Mo. Okay! I have to do it. Just be ready to hold me when it's over. I'll be in town with Jamie, and of course, our parents won't know about you. They'll just have to absorb the shock of our divorce for now. Our relationship will come later when they've recovered a bit. Oh, I almost forgot, Jamie said he wanted to try your bungee jump concession. Maybe we can do that the day after we arrive. I'll fake it until after that before I make my announcement."

"Sounds good to me, honey. I can't believe we're finally on our way to making this happen."

Chapter Eighty-Eight

The plane landed at noon. Jamie's parents, now retired, met them at the airport and headed off to Salmon. This time, the trip seemed quieter than usual. After the first half hour, there was little spoken until they were at the Duncans' front door. Emma's parents were waiting for them there, and then the discussion picked up, including much hub-bub over Jamie's "leap of faith."

"Have you ever bungee jumped before?" asked Emma's dad.

"Nope," said Jamie, "but I've watched others do it and always wanted to give it a try. And with old Mo running the operation, I'm sure it will be safe."

"Of course it will," chimed in Emma.

Then Emma's mom added that they should all come over to her house for an early dinner because the next day was going to be so busy, with an early start. They finally decided to meet the next morning for breakfast at the local diner and then head over to the bridge for the jump that Jamie had scheduled for 10:00 a.m.

It was 2:00 a.m. when a figure dressed all in black slith-ered down toward the bridge. The sidewalks in Salmon gen-erally rolled up at 10:00 in the evening, so things were both dark and very quiet. In just minutes, this person achieved a spot on the undercarriage of the bridge where the rubber strands of the bungee jump were fastened. A flash of light sprang from the blade as it severed the rubber to within one inch of its six inch width. A small piece of clear tape was then fastened to the back of it so that it appeared to be as solid as ever. Then, as quickly and quietly as this had happened, it was over.

The morning came with perfect weather. It was seventy degrees at sunrise and almost eighty degrees when they arrived at the bridge. While other customers were waiting in line for the jump, a sign had been posted stating that the first jump was to be at 10:00 a.m. and that it was reserved for a Salmon native and former hero of the Salmon Savages high school football team. Many knew Jamie personally, and some of the younger folks had even heard about his exploits on the gridiron.

When the Steele's SUV arrived at the bridge, the whole family jumped out, very excited (though a little nervous) about what was about to transpire. Jamie excused himself briefly, saying he needed to use the men's room before the jump. He ran over to the restrooms, where he knew Stu would be waiting for him in a stall. He quickly dropped his suit while Stu fastened a small canister with a valve to his inner thigh. He then connected a breathing tube to the canister and taped it to Jamie's chest. Jamie had worn a loose-fitting long bathing suit and T-shirt so none of this could be seen as he returned to the bridge. It was just two minutes before 10:00 when he climbed up on the bridge railing and positioned himself to jump. Emma came over, and Jamie bent down to give her a quick kiss. Mo asked if he was ready, and Jamie gave him the okay.

When the *snap* came, and he hit the water, dread was on everyone's face. The crowd rushed off the bridge to the shore to see where or if he would come up. They all knew about the rocks and the direction of the current, so they all came to the same part of the shore. When after several seconds he didn't come up, they began to walk along the riverbank in the direction of the current—and away from Jamie.

When he was in school, Jamie and the boys had often gone swimming in this area. When Jamie decided on his plan, he knew where Mo was likely to place the bungee cord to control jumpers' point of entry into the water. There was a sudden drop at that point that went from six feet deep to more than twenty feet, where he could safely land. When he jumped, he angled himself sufficiently to miss—barely miss—the rocks and land in the deep water. Because the river was not too wide at that point, he knew he could swim against the current to the other side as long as he had enough air to stay out of sight until the crowd left the immediate area. One of his CIA cohorts would meet him on the other side, cover him quickly with a large tarp, and drop him into the back of a waiting station wagon. It worked like a charm.

Chapter Eighty-Nine

Fright was on everyone's face. Jamie's parents were devastated. Emma's folks ran to the nearby garage where they kept their rowboat and dropped it in the river to start a search. The local police checked the area where the bungee cord had been attached. The clean-cut and remnant of the tape caused immediate suspicion of foul play. Mohammed, though well-known to everyone, was segregated from the crowd and brought back to the bridge to look at the evidence and be questioned about what had happened. Emma stayed with the Duncans as they all attempted to stay calm.

While everyone else kept their eyes on the river, Jamie took a short drive to a safe house the CIA had rented. The home was located in an unincorporated area just outside the Salmon city limits. It had been up for sale for months. The FOR SALE sign had been removed. While the house would only be in use for a few days, it allowed them a place for security while the plan they had devised played itself out.

From the time Jamie escaped the river until his arrival at the house, only eight minutes passed. He quickly showered and changed into dry jeans and a T-shirt. He picked up his mobile radio and contacted Stu, who was carefully observing the activities in town and watching, in particular, to see if there was any obvious result from the ongoing questioning of Mohammed or if there were any possible sightings of Ali Hassan or Mohammed's father.

*****

It didn't take long, but it came by phone intercept back in New York instead of a visual in town. The call came from the senior Mr. Amsur to Ali. He had been at home during the jump. His home was not far from the bridge, and when he heard the commotion, he had become concerned. Knowing his son would be at the bridge and out of contact, he called Ali to find out what had happened. When Ali told him he had seen Mo being escorted to the police station, his father's heart rate spiked.

"What happened, Ali?" he gasped.

"The Duncan boy jumped and the bungee cord gave way. Everyone is in panic. Obviously, with Mo owning the concession, they had to question him."

"You're sure, Ali? It couldn't have anything to do with IGO, could it? Remember, Duncan is with the CIA!"

"I can't imagine why, my friend. Just relax. I'll take a walk and see If I can learn anything. I don't want you stressing your heart over nothing."

A reference to IGO was just one more nail in the coffin for the small group of Salmon conspirators. As soon as this call was picked up, Stu was alerted. He immediately moved toward Ali's office. As he came close, he saw Ali coming out and heading toward the police station. He followed him along the sidewalk, getting closer with each step.

When Ali stopped to talk with a deputy standing in front of the station, he also stopped, lit a cigarette, and listened to the conversation.

The two men obviously knew each other well. The deputy implied there was more to the questioning than what he would have expected. It seemed that a new person that the deputy had never seen before was in a closed-door room with the sheriff talking to Mohammed. The desk clerk said he thought he heard the man ID himself as a member of the CIA but wasn't sure. When Ali heard this, he quickly thanked the deputy, turned back toward his office, and took off at a rapid pace. His face had turned an ashen white.

Suddenly, he found himself blocked on the sidewalk by Stu's imposing figure. "Excuse me, Mr. Hassan," said Stu, "I must talk to you."

"And who might you be?" responded Ali.

"This is who I am," said Stu as he presented his CIA credential. "Why don't we have a chat in your office?"

"I don't understand," said Ali. "Have I done something inappropriate?"

"Well, that's what we're about to discuss, sir. Let's go."

*****

While they walked the short distance to Ali's base of operations, Mohammed was being grilled in a way he certainly hadn't expected. They had started the interrogation discussing the jump cord but gradually switched over to questions totally unrelated to the day's events. They began to ask if he knew a man by the name of Ali Hassan.

"I do know him," he responded. "He is my father's best friend."

"How long have you known him?"

"Ever since my dad encouraged him to move here from Canada. I was in high school at the time, so it's around sixteen–seventeen years or so."

"Have you had anything to do with him other than to have a friendly relationship with the man?"

"Not really," said Mo, as he began to be quite concerned over the direction of the questioning.

"Have you ever heard of a group known as IGO?" asked the man in the room whom he hadn't seen before.

"Wait a minute," said Mo. "I thought we were here because of the horrible accident that just took place today. That was my oldest friend that crashed into the river. Shouldn't we be concerning ourselves with him?"

"Of course, Mr. Amsur, but there's more than one side to this story, and part of it has to do with this IGO group. So again, I'll ask you, do you know anything about IGO? Remember, you want to be completely truthful."

Mohammed's heart was pounding so hard he thought his chest would soon explode. His father's face and that of Ali played through his mind's eye. He knew there could be only one answer.

"No, I know nothing of this group."

"I see," was the emotionless response from his questioner. "Please keep yourself available, Mr. Amsur. I'm sure there will be more questions as our investigation progresses.

I must insist that you not leave town until we advise you further. Sheriff Nelson will be in touch with you soon. Thank you for your cooperation."

Chapter Ninety

Hours had passed, and hope for Jamie's survival was quickly fading. The Steeles had traveled three miles downriver and finally decided that if he hadn't come up yet, he was surely lost. The Duncans were inconsolable, and Emma, despite her affair with Mo, had never wanted anything like this to happen.

Emma excused herself from the Duncans, saying that she would have to drive her parents' truck downriver to pick them up and return the boat to the dock. As she left, Sheriff Nelson, who had also befriended the Duncans, showed up and drove them home to wait for further news. Jamie knew this would be a horrible time for his folks but rationalized it to himself as he knew it wouldn't last long.

As soon as Emma had returned her parents to town, they rushed over to the Duncans'. Emma said she would be right along but wanted to see Mo first to find out more about what had happened.

She ran to his shop, but the door was locked. She pounded on the door, and a few moments later, Mohammed raised the shade, saw who it was, and quickly opened the door, shutting and locking it behind Emma just as quickly. He grabbed Emma and held on for dear life. Emma leaned back and saw he had been crying.

"Oh, Em," he blurted, "I can't believe this. We both wanted Jamie to start another life and be out of ours, but not like this."

"I'm so glad you said that, Mo. I couldn't imagine you being involved in this tragedy, but I had to be sure."

"I know, Em. You had the right to be suspect, but if anyone knows me well, it is you, and you know I could never contemplate such a thing, let alone act on it. But I did learn from the sheriff that there was intent by someone. The bungee cord had been cut almost completely through and then taped together to give the appearance of being intact. I'm sure they suspect me because it was my con-cession, but they certainly can't prove anything. However, there is one more thing that is of concern. I had planned to talk to you about it when we were together in New York, but I guess I never got around to it. It is an uncomfortable subject, but in all fairness to you, if we are to spend the rest of our lives together, you must know about it."

Mo went on in detail to tell Emma about IGO, how he became involved, and how the CIA had become suspi-cious. He also told her about the session he had just been through with the sheriff and the CIA agent and how the direction of his questioning had moved to IGO. It was a lot for Emma to take in, especially with the overriding sorrow of the day's events. Had she known earlier, she would have been better able to absorb it all. Now she couldn't seem to take it all in. It just seemed as though her dear Mo was telling her he was a traitor to his country. She just sat there, mouth agape, staring at the wall, and not knowing what to say or do.

Finally, she took a step back from Mo and said, "Honey, I need some time to digest what you just told me. I think I'd better get back to the Duncans' house for now. I would tell you to come, but I don't know how they would react at this moment. I think it might be too raw for them right now. Why don't you go home and just stay there for now? I'll call you tonight or tomorrow morning to update you on what's going on there. I'll also let them know you're just devastated and that you need time to get yourself together before you come to see them."

Without so much as a hug, Emma turned and left the shop. She and Mo were each left alone with their thoughts.

Chapter Ninety-One

Jamie, Stu, and the Iranian interrogator listened carefully to the recording of Mo's questioning. When he denied knowledge of IGO, they knew he was lying and that they had him on charges of treason and likely more. His father and Hassan were also ready for arrest on money-laundering charges along with treason and fraud as they had misrepresented the true goal of their charity. Others who might be involved—including US citizens the CIA might be able to prove made contributions to IGO—may be eligible for charges of treason as well. Now the question was when to make the arrests.

It took a few days to put all the evidence in order and send it to Langley. While they waited, Jamie had to remain incommunicado. Finally, the word came back to proceed.

It was 7:00 a.m. Stu and one of his assistants appeared at Mo's shop just as he was unlocking the door. Jamie had asked Stu to handle this because of his long relationship with Mo. As he was about to push the door open, Mo looked up at Stu, his imposing 6' 6" figure casting a long shadow over his target.

"Mr. Amsur, my name is Stu Johnson. I'm the supervising agent on the IGO case. I must ask that you come with me to the sheriff's office."

"But I must open my shop," replied Mo in his meekest voice.

"I'm afraid your shop may not be operating today unless you have an employee to handle it. And I might add, you should probably be thinking about how it will be operating for a number of years to come. In that context, it might be best for you to sell the entire operation. You see, Mr. Amsur, I'm placing you under arrest for the crimes of money-laundering, fraud, and treason."

With this, Stu read him his rights and suggested he would need to obtain a lawyer for his defense.

Mo was dumbstruck. He relocked the door to his shop and proceeded to the sheriff's office without another word. When he arrived, he was struck with another shock. There stood Jamie with Ali Hassan and his father, both seated on a bench with their heads hanging down.

"Jamie, this is crazy!" shouted Mo. "How could you do this to us?"

"You did it to yourself, Mo. All three of you. I couldn't believe it myself until I saw the proof. It is a sad day when your oldest friend turns out to be a traitor." *In more ways than one*, Jamie thought to himself.

The three men were formally booked and placed in a holding cell as preparations were made to transfer them to Washington for a federal trial. While these details were being handled, Jamie rushed to his parents' home. He rang the bell. Emma opened the door, and when she saw Jamie, she nearly fainted.

"My god, Jamie, it's been a week! Where have you been? What's going on?"

Before he could answer, his mom and dad were at the door. From the depths of despair, they reached for their son and hugged him so fiercely he almost collapsed under the weight of their passion.

After the first burst of emotion, Emma, the Duncans, and the Steeles retreated to the living room, where Jamie was able to tell them the basics of what was going on.

"Well," he started, "I am so sorry for having put you through this, and you're all going to be shocked by what I have to tell you, especially you, Em, since both of us have been so close to Mohammed for so many years."

Emma's face went pale. The four parents had very quizzical looks on their faces. Jamie went on. "For some time, the CIA has been suspicious of a group known as IGO. They were set up as a charity committed to the support of the US military. And they did, in fact, contribute small amounts to the Department of Defense, primarily for the benefit of wounded troops. However, that money was a pittance compared to the funds they laundered through a Canadian bank that was actually connected to Iran. In other words, their true purpose was to finance the Iranian government. As you know, contributions to that government under current US law are considered to be treasonous. Well, as it turns out, Mo's dad, his best friend, Ali Hassan, and Mo himself were IGO. And we've just arrested all three of them. The jump I made was just a ruse to get some needed evidence. I suspect you'll not see any of them for many years, if ever again."

As he said this, he looked squarely at Emma, whom he could tell was straining to hold in her emotions. Tears were welling up, and finally, she escaped the room without a word.

Jamie's dad spoke up, saying he didn't know Mo's dad or Ali Hassan very well but was just sick that Mo was caught up in all this. Jamie agreed but said nothing of Mo's relationship with Emma—that he would save for Emma when they were finally alone.

Chapter Ninety-Two

When Emma left the Duncans' living room, she quickly exited the house through the back door and ran to her parents' home. Her face had turned a deep red that was flush with tears as she sobbed openly all the way to her bedroom, where she locked the door.

Soon after, Jamie excused himself, saying he understood how upset Emma must be at the news about Mo and wanted to see if he could help.

He ran back to the Steeles' house and could hear Emma crying through her bedroom door. He knocked softly but received no reply. When he tried again, Emma screamed, "Leave me alone! Leave me alone!"

Not sure of the best approach given her emotions, Jamie decided to wait until Emma calmed down a bit. She didn't leave her room until three hours later when her need for the bathroom could no longer be contained. Her parents were still at the Duncans'. When she saw Jamie sitting in the living room, she tiptoed across the hall. He had heard her but didn't move. After she locked herself in the bathroom, he walked quietly down the hall and positioned himself across from the bathroom door. As soon as she opened the door and saw him, she tried to retreat. He stepped across the hall and held the door open.

"Emma," he said, "I understand your concern about Mo's future, but having heard what he has done, don't you have to put things into perspective? Look, I feel bad that my oldest friend is in this kind of trouble, but he did it to himself. In other words, I feel the same emotions you do, but they are mitigated by the realities of the situation. You, on the other hand, seem to be taking the situation much more to heart. Perhaps there's something else between you two that I'm not aware of. Tell me, is there something else I should know?"

Emma's face again began to redden. She looked at Jamie and started to say something but then seemed unable to get it out. She then took a step toward her room. As she did, Jamie grabbed her arm and held her firmly.

"Talk to me, Em," he said. "Your reaction is extreme to the point that you're giving me real concern."

"I don't have anything to say to you!" Emma yelled, pulling her arm free.

Jamie stopped her from closing her bedroom door. She jumped into her bed, pulled the covers over her head, and assumed the fetal position.

"You can run, and you can try to hide, Em, but you won't succeed. Since you won't tell me anything, then I'll tell you. I became suspicious of yours and Mo's relationship on our last trip here when you came toward me from the back office of Mo's shop needing to straighten your clothes and replace the lipstick you had just put on before we came to visit. Mo was a bit disheveled too. I elected to let that pass at the time, but when we started to get into the IGO investigation, I wanted to be sure Mo wasn't involved. I certainly didn't want him to be arrested if he wasn't a player. So I received a court order to tap his phone. Soon after, I came home to find a tape of a call between him and a lady with a very familiar voice expressing her love for him and a yearning to see him as soon as possible. It was then that I knew for sure that the two of you were having an affair. And then, to further confirm your relationship, there was that incredible chance meeting with Soya, who has been living here under a new identity. How ironic, I thought, that you and your Iranian lover should meet up with one of the very few people in New York that you would know."

Emma, still under the covers, opened her eyes. *Why has Jamie been in touch with Soya? He never mentioned he knew her new location or name and certainly not that they had been in touch.*

Finally, she mustered up enough courage to speak. "Jamie, why have you been in touch with Soya? I thought her new identity and location were to be kept secret."

Jamie paused and then responded, "I've been in contact with her only because I met her by chance one night at the Four Seasons restaurant. She had been at an office party there and saw me having dinner as she was leaving. She stopped to thank me for all the help I had given her and gave me her new name on the QT. We also exchanged contact information. After she saw you that day at the museum, she gave me a call to let me know something hadn't seemed right about the way you were acting...or about your having a strange gentleman friend with you while I was out of town."

Jamie paused again and continued, "In any event, we're not here to talk about her. We're here to talk about you and your affair and your plan to divorce me and marry Mo. Maybe we should have a friendly chat this evening with your folks about their All-American girl, whose honesty now must be called into question. I'm sure they'd be thrilled to hear your side of this story, as would my folks. It's a sweet little package you've wrapped up for everybody in the family. And think of the townsfolk, all of whom will know within twenty-four hours once news of your little scandal breaks. You'll be the talk of the town, but not in the way you once were. So are you ready to come out from under the covers and face your husband? You know you can't stay there forever."

The covers moved. Slowly Emma's face emerged. It was still flush, but the tears had dried, and she simply wore a stunned look. Finally, she said in a meek voice, "You wouldn't dare tell them. I know you can be very mean, but I don't think you would want to cause such hurt to them. I know it's my fault, so why not find a way to hurt me? But not them. Please, I beg you."

"And how would you like to handle the news of our pending divorce? I can assure you that that is the future of our marriage now that I know the whole story. How and when would you like to break this wonderful news to our parents?"

"I don't know. Please let me work it out in my head before you do anything rash. Once I get myself together, I promise I'll make the announcement and find a way to put the blame on me. Let's go back to New York first and give me a couple of weeks to work it out. I won't be long, I promise."

"Okay, Em. A couple of weeks, but that's it. It's time we got on with our lives."

Chapter Ninety-Three

The IGO trio was in federal prison awaiting formal court procedures. Bail was not allowed as the Justice Department claimed the men would be likely flight risks.

Emma struggled tremendously as she sought the right words to explain the tragedy of a lost marriage while never indicating she and Mo had been involved in an affair. All she could think of, it seemed, was poor Mo sitting in prison, having no desire to participate in IGO in the first place. She just wanted to take his father and Ali Hassan and make them take all the blame so Mo could go free. The truth was that they would willingly comply with this wish if only it could be done. But it couldn't. There was too much direct evidence against Mo.

As time was winding down on her promise to Jamie, Emma decided to go for a walk just to clear her head. She strolled for hours, tossing words back and forth as she tried to simulate the conversation she would have with her folks. As she was on her way back to the apartment, she approached the hotel where she used to make her secret calls to Mo. She decided to go in to buy a bottle of water as she had become thirsty from the walk. She passed through the lobby, and as she passed the phone booth she had used so many times, she saw the backside of a familiar figure, wearing a Stanford T-shirt. She knew at once it was Jamie. Because he couldn't see her, she was able to enter the adjacent phone booth and shut the door. She could hear his voice rather clearly. When the name Soya popped up, she drew her ear closer to the wall separating the two phone booths. Five minutes later, the call ended, and life had just become much different for her.

Jamie left the booth. Emma didn't move until he had time enough to leave the hotel.

When she finally exited, she could see him a block away, almost to the entry of their apartment building. Her old thoughts were supplanted by some that gave her new leverage and a feeling of justification, or at least equality in this personal tragedy. It was time, while all was fresh in her mind, to deal the equalizing blow.

She and Jamie showered. It was almost time for dinner, but Jamie noticed nothing had been prepared. He approached Emma and asked, "Are you planning to make dinner, or are we on our own tonight?"

"I'm afraid it's the latter, but there's something we must discuss first. What I have to say is quite important relative to our situation and will surely give you something to 'chew on' as you have your solo dinner this evening."

"Does that mean you've finally figured out what to say to the folks?"

"Well, I had been getting very close to that point when something happened that could affect our approach."

"Our approach? I believe we agreed that this deal was all yours."

"That's right, except something happened today that changed that perspective."

"And what might that be?"

"Let's call it a bit of coincidence. You see, I was out for a long walk today, trying to sort out how to tell my folks. I had gotten thirsty and stopped in the little hotel down the street to get a bottle of water. As I walked through the lobby toward their little shop, I saw a familiar figure in a phone booth that just happened to be wearing his very old Stanford T-shirt. First, that's the same phone booth I used to use to call Mo. The very same booth from which I made the call you taped. And there you were, just like me, calling your Iranian lover, the now-famous Soya. I had the privilege of hearing your very romantic conversation about your plans for a future together, the way you couldn't wait to be a dad to her boys, and how you would love to adopt them as your own. How perfect, Jamie, that each of us was doing the same thing to each other with our Iranian friends. I can just imagine how your boss, Stu, will react when he finds out who you are involved with. Yes, I am guilty, and I definitely feel the guilt, but you are right there with me, my dear husband, and so now we're going to suffer through our parental presentation together. Am I clear?"

Jamie sat, stunned. He knew she was right, and he just felt the guilt pour out all over him.

Chapter Ninety-Four

Jamie had to think. He had to be alone. He grabbed an overnight bag, threw in a change of clothes, and a dopp kit, and headed to a nearby motel. Once ensconced, he called Soya at work and explained what had just happened and that he would have to go through the agony of parental explanation. The how and why of it all was something he was trying to work out in his head. He told her how he ached to see her and feel reassurance from her that it would all work out for the best.

"Of course it will," she said. "Why don't you come over a little later after the boys have gone to bed, and we can work out the best approach together?"

"Thanks, honey," he replied. "I was hoping you would say that. I'll come out around 9:30 or 10:00."

As Jamie drove toward the suburbs to see Soya, he was listening to the local news channel, barely paying attention to it until a special announcement interrupted the regular programming.

"Ladies and gentlemen, we are interrupting our regularly scheduled newscast to report what appears to be a violent gas explosion that has completely destroyed one home and seriously damaged a neighboring building. Helicopters have been sent to film the resulting fire while trucks from three local villages have been sent to douse the blaze. We will report further as more details become known. Now back to our regular program."

Jamie was within a mile of Soya's house and began to see an orange glow in the sky. As he drew closer, the light from the apparent fire intensified. Two blocks from Soya's home, all traffic was being detoured. Jamie pulled over on a side street and began to run toward Soya's house, which was in the direction of the flames. And then he knew. She was gone. The boys were gone. His new life-to-be was gone.

He stopped a policeman and asked what had happened. The officer responded that they originally had thought it was a gas explosion, but the first inspector on the scene said it didn't look that way. He thought C4 explosives had been set in a way and in an amount to assure total destruction. Casualties, if any, were not yet known.

Jamie knew after hearing this comment, which confirmed his initial suspicion that the Iranians had somehow been able to track down Soya and further complete the assassination that had taken Samir and the others, leaving only Ibrahim's family.

Jamie also knew a fire of this intensity would likely leave nothing but ash behind. He couldn't bear the thought of the firemen searching through the debris for bodies, and he certainly didn't want to be there and have to explain his presence. He walked quickly to his car and returned to his motel room. Now, he thought, both he and Emma had lost their loves and had only themselves to blame. *What a mess*, he thought to himself.

Jamie grabbed his dopp kit and removed the bottle of sleeping pills he had been using in the midst of all the turmoil in his life. He stared at the label and thought again of Soya and the three sweet boys he knew had perished. Never a crier in his life, he suddenly burst into tears and then heavy, uncontrolled sobs. His body began to shake as he held his head in his hands in a state of total desperation. Finally, he looked again at the bottle and ran into the bathroom. He grabbed a glass, filled it with water and then in a flash downed the entire bottle of pills.

He returned to the bed, still sobbing until the pills overtook him. He lost consciousness and lay still, never to wake again.

*****

After Jamie's funeral, Emma packed up their apartment in New York and moved back to Salmon, where she spent the rest of her life teaching the first graders she loved years before. But that smile that had always lit up the room was never seen again.

CPSIA information can be obtained
at www.ICGtesting.com
Printed in the USA
LVHW040903181020
669076LV00002B/400

9 781645 845898